THE TRAIL OF THE SERPENT

BOOKS BY Jan de Hartog

PLAYS

JAN DE HARTOG

THE TRAIL OF THE SERPENT

A Cornelia & Michael Bessie Book

HARPER & ROW, PUBLISHERS, New York
Cambridge, Philadelphia, San Francisco, London
Mexico City, São Paulo, Sydney

1817

FIRST EDITION

Designer: Sidney Feinberg

This book is set in 10½-point Linotron 202 Souvenir Light. It was composed by Fisher Composition, Inc., New York, and printed and bound by R. R. Donnelley and Sons Company, the Lakeside Press, Chicago.

Library of Congress Cataloging in Publication Data

Hartog, Jan de, 1914–
  The trail of the serpent.
  I. Title.
PR6015.A674T7   1983   813'.54   80-8228
ISBN 0-06-010983-1

---

83 84 85 86 87 10 9 8 7 6 5 4 3 2 1

CONTENTS

Some flow'rets of Eden ye still inherit,
But the trail of the Serpent is over them all.

THOMAS MOORE
(1779–1852)

PROLOGUE

This is the story as it is still being told among the rapidly diminishing numbers of ex-colonials who survived the collapse of the Dutch empire during the Second World War. It has, by now, acquired the aura of a fable.

To us, the witty young esthete lost in the mountains, the martyred nun, the midget captain with his atheist dog seem like creatures of legend; yet it is only yesterday that they and others like them ruled an empire the size of the United States, which had been under the Dutch flag for over three centuries. It was an empire on which the sun never set, as, indeed, it never set on the British, the French or the Portuguese. Lost empires all, lost shadows of great characters and wondrous deeds, as antique now as the Wars of the Roses.

This, then, is the story of Captain Krasser, Sister Ursula and Herman Winsum, M.A., as it can still be heard in the musty clubs of The Hague and Amsterdam where the survivors of the colonial days gather.

It is based on a true incident. Its main characters, all dead now, lived their wild and noble lives in an alien world their ancestors had conquered for them and which they lost, in one unimaginable cataclysm, in the distant year of 1942.

PART ONE

The Fall

1   War came to the Dutch East Indies in late 1941. Pearl Harbor was attacked on December 7, Queen Wilhelmina of the Netherlands declared war on Japan the day after; but during the first weeks of the Pacific War it appeared the Japanese were headed for Singapore and Australia, bypassing the Dutch East Indies. They certainly did not seem to be interested in the island of Borneo.

The day the Japanese landed in Sarawak on the British north coast of the island, Herman Winsum, M.A., youthful editor for religion and arts of the *Borneo Times,* found himself a hundred miles inland in the oil town of Rauwatta. He had come over from Banjermasin the day before to review a performance of *The Importance of Being Earnest* by the local amateur theatrical society.

At the moment of the invasion Herman was discussing the layout of the theater page for the weekend edition with a Mrs. Josephine Bohm, local stringer for the paper. The manager of the Hôtel des Indes had given them the conference room for the morning to work in, as it had a large table on which to spread out their photographs, and he kept them supplied with an endless round of miniature glasses of ice-cold Dutch gin, a service for which the hotel was justly famous.

Mrs. Bohm was, so Herman assumed, a so-called oil wife with plenty of time to care for herself with hedonistic dedication. She was a statuesque blonde in her thirties, too ample for his taste; he had a predilection for the women of Modigliani. She wore a white sharkskin suit, sheer white stockings and a string of pearls, obviously real, which plumbed tantalizingly the depths of her cleavage. Her Delft-blue eyes, set wide apart, observed him with sidelong glances that, after their fourth miniature glass of ice-cold gin, became somewhat unnerving. But she was professional enough; she proved to be well versed in local gossip and produced a sheaf of spicily scandalous candids of the Rauwatta *beau monde*. "Rather than stills of the cast," she ventured, "my guess is that what the readers want to see is who escorted whom to the first night, and which wife was caught snarling at her husband's leer at someone else's wife."

Herman shuffled the photographs, obviously taken during a party after the performance. They showed couples with funny hats and Halloween noses, everyone holding a glass; spirits must have flowed freely and loosened inhibitions. For some reason, however, the pictures evoked not a happy get-together after an evening in the theater, but the dark menace of the jungle surrounding the prim little town, the hot, humid air charged with fecundity, the steamy dawns, the thunderous dusks. There was something of the *Decameron* about them, an atmosphere of forced revelry in a plague-ridden town. "Fascinating," Herman said. "Did you take these yourself?"

Mrs. Bohm nodded with a self-satisfied smile.

"Amazing they allowed you to take them—this one, for instance." The photograph showed an overweight male in his late

8

forties, flushed with booze and crowned with a beanie with pro-peller, slavering over a girl no older than seventeen, who peered into his mouth as if invited to have a look at his uvula. "How did you manage to get it?"

She gave him one of her sidelong glances, then, to his star-tled surprise, pulled the string of pearls out of her cleavage, slowly, like an angler winding in a trout, and produced a small camera dangling at the end of it. "With this," she said.

"My God! What's that?"

"Japanese. It's the kind spies use."

Herman took the malevolent-looking little thing in his hand and was struck by its warmth. It gave him a *frisson* of sensuous excitement. Surprisingly so; he had always looked upon the usual male preference for heavy breasts as a throwback to baby-hood. "Well," he said, with a hint of irritation, "fascinating as they may be, Mrs.—er—Bohm, I'm afraid I won't be able to use them. I'm supposed to illustrate the review of a play in the arts section, not an item in the gossip column."

"As you wish," she said, with odd passivity. "You're the edi-tor." She sat down on a corner of the table, one leg dangling, showing a knee, round and rosy in a demure white silk stocking which somehow made it look brazenly exposed. It was a miracle she had managed to keep her skin so peachlike in the tropics. It also was a miracle that in what, according to her photographs, appeared to be a primeval jungle drunk with lust she had re-tained the unruffled passivity of an Impressionist milkmaid. Renoir no doubt would have painted her as *Nude in Field of Buttercups,* surrounded by masticating cows. He felt he had been rather brusque. "I'd like to hang on to them, though. For some future essay. Something in the nature of *Last Orgy in Pompeii.*"

At a later date these flippant words would take on the awe-some portent of a flash of precognition; at the moment, as he looked up at her, he realized that to her they represented the depth of infantilism. It triggered a motherly response in her which made her put an arm of surprising weight around his neck and kiss him squarely on the lips. He struggled, totally surprised and prissily outraged, with a hint of small-animal panic; but she drew all resistance, all independence out of him with calm determination, as if drinking creamy milk from a dipper in a long, uninterrupted draft.

As in all bad movies, this was the moment the hotel manager burst into the room with the news that the Japanese had invaded Borneo. Despite his embarrassment at being discovered *in flagrante,* Herman was struck by the expression on the manager's face as the man shouted, "War! It's war! The Japs are bombing Tarakan! They're landing troops in Sarawak!" His voice expressed horror, but his face sensual excitement.

Herman felt a strange clarity come over him, a sense of awakening, as if these last two years he had lived in a dream. He had been haunted by the specter of war ever since his student days. He had turned down the lucrative and prestigious post of curator of a private Van Gogh museum in the Dutch provinces only to escape the encroaching shadow of war. He had taken on the assignment of Arts and Religious Editor of an abysmally provincial journal in the farthest-flung outpost of the Dutch East Indies only as a joke, as far as his friends were concerned: "Art" didn't exist below Gibraltar, and he deserved the epithet "religious" only insofar as, for his Master's, he had written as the obligatory second subject a learned but tongue-in-cheek essay on archetypal symbolisms in the Song of Solomon. In actual fact, however, his acceptance of the assignment had not been a joke: in Borneo, he had assumed, he would at least be safe from the impending war. Now, here it was: his appointment in Samarra.

Mrs. Bohm's reaction to the manager's message of doom was different. It did not seem to ruffle her at all. She sat cool, white and tranquil amidst the suddenly pathetic photographs of the reveling first-nighters with a faraway look on her face, as if listening to distant music.

After the manager darted out to carry the seed of panic farther on his flight she briefly touched Herman's cheek and said, "Well, you'd better go and see Major Benstra while I try to get hold of Sam Hendriks." She sounded totally in control; Herman was struck by the thought that if anyone could save the Dutch East Indies it was Mrs. Bohm. What would be needed now was fast, lucid thinking by very cool heads.

"Major Benstra?" he asked. "Who's he?"

"The ranking military officer in the district," she replied, sliding off the table. "Go in your capacity of editor of the *Times*. Ask for information on the condition of the roads leading out of town. We can expect air raids; maybe the Japs will send a gunboat upriver to shell the town. We'll have to get the hell out of here."

"But surely the Japanese won't be here for hours!" he exclaimed. "Days!"

"My guess is they will," she said, collecting her photographs, an impressive display of orderliness. "I've lived through this before. My husband was stationed in Shanghai when the Japs bombed the town. They have a knack of jumping before they look. So, off with you."

She seemed so calm, so in control, yet her words caused a tremor of panic. He pushed his chair under the table and said, with an effort at sounding casual, "If you insist. Where do I find this Benstra?"

"In Government House. Throw your weight around, take his picture. He's a fatuous ass, but he has a fleet of cars. Get us some transportation."

"I'll do my best." He went toward the door, where he turned and asked, "Will we be seeing each other again?"

She smiled. "Of course we will. We'll beat them to the punch together, Manny."

No one had ever called him by that nauseating name. Yet he heard himself ask, like a character in a French farce, "But what about your husband?"

She slipped the photographs into their envelope. "In the Army. Somewhere in Java." She gave him another of her unnerving sidelong glances. "And you? Married?"

"Engaged."

"Where is she?"

"In Holland. Occupied by the Germans." It was a ridiculous thing to say. In an effort to escape from the French farce, he added, "Her name is Isabel."

"H'm," Mrs. Bohm said, looking at his mouth, thereby somehow disposing of his fiancée's ineffectual ghost. "Major Benstra. Government House."

He opened the door. "Where shall we meet?"

She smiled. "Don't worry, Manny. I'll know where to find you."

Bewildered by the enigma of her attraction, he fled.

2

As Herman set out for Government House, the shaded streets of Rauwatta were empty and somnolently quiet.

From the verandas of some of the bungalows radio music blared, occasionally interrupted by the voice of a news announcer. No one was running in panic; Herman felt conspicuous in his solitary urgency and walked on with a measured stride. He still experienced that feeling of relief, but was no longer sure whether it was caused by the war catching up with him or by Mrs. Bohm's assault and its implications. She had been doing something exciting with her tongue just when the manager burst into the conference room. He felt the impulse to make a boyish leap under the trees and slap his behind. For years the mere thought of war had choked him with paranoid fear; now, thanks to Mrs. Bohm, he felt like a liberated prisoner. The whole thing was crazy. So was she. Maybe they all were. Maybe that was what war was: communal insanity.

Government House, a neo-Grecian pile with whitewashed

stucco pillars, turned out to be situated in a parklike enclosure. At the gate, two native soldiers in white helmets stood guard, staring fixedly ahead as Herman self-consciously made his way between them, not knowing whether to smile, salute or look grave and preoccupied. As he strode up the white gravel drive to the steps of the building, bees hummed in cambodja trees heavy with voluptuous blooms after the rains of the wet monsoon. A peacock shrieked unmelodiously among the azaleas on the lawn and spread the quivering, narcissistic glory of its tail. On the pillars of the façade, chi-chacks dashed about like clockwork lizards; under the eaves, pigeons were roosting, covering the tiled floor of the entrance with their traces. It seemed inconceivable that anything as brutal and chaotic as war could disturb the sleepy peace of this outpost of the Dutch empire. The white man had been here since the early 1600's and there was no reason why he should not stay here for another three centuries, at the end of which Government House in Rauwatta would stand among these dark blue trees exactly as it stood now, Roman outpost in the jungle of Gaul.

A native corporal led him down a cool corridor with numbered doors, behind which typewriters clattered and telephones rang. There was not a trace of urgency in the air; for the first time the possibility occurred to him that the Dutch Army might keep the Japanese at bay.

Major Benstra, seated behind a desk full of telephones, letter trays, a fan and a portrait in a silver frame, seemed unfazed by the emergency. On the wall, a picture of Queen Wilhelmina gazed down upon his visitor with a look of majestic disapproval. On the opposite wall was a map of the Dutch East Indies, full of red markers that seemed to indicate a military might unsuspected by the enemy. Against the major's desk leaned a tasseled saber, romantic remnant of more chivalrous times. The major himself was exactly as Mrs. Bohm had described him; Herman detested him at sight.

As usual, this turned out to be mutual; as he introduced himself, Herman caught the major looking at him like a butcher appraising a calf. "And what can I do for you, sir?"

"It's about the Japanese invasion," Herman said, with again the feeling of taking part in a French farce.

"What about it?"

"I wonder if you could tell me what the situation is around Rauwatta. Access roads, and so on. I'd like to telephone the information through to my paper in Banjermasin."

"Now come, come, young man," the major said condescendingly. "As a newspaperman, you should know better than to ask for classified information."

"Very well. How about transportation? It is essential that I get back to my desk in Banjermasin as fast as possible and I wonder if you would help me there."

"How?"

"Well—a car?"

The major looked at him with distaste. "What's the hurry, may I ask? All trains are running normally and on schedule. The last thing we want is an atmosphere of panic among the civilian population."

"Of course," Herman said, eager now to get away. "So you don't expect any air raids?"

"Air raids?" the major asked contemptuously. "Nonsense! Not a single plane will get through. Now if you'll excuse me . . ."

"Certainly," Herman said. "Good day."

He had his hand on the knob of the door when suddenly it was violently thrust open, knocking him backward against the major's desk. At first he thought some idiot must have crashed in with an urgent message; then he thought of a boiler explosion; then, outside, a high-pitched whine came shrieking down, followed by a colossal concussion which showered plaster and glass in the corridor and set women's voices screaming behind doors. His mind was numbed, but his body reacted with a flash-like reflex. He saw the major dive under his desk; in one sinuous bound, of which he would never have thought himself capable, he leaped across it to join the cowering man in the little dark cavity underneath. There they sat, pressed close together, while bombs came shrieking down and exploded with ear-splitting concussions all around them. Herman smelled sweat and men's deodorant and was overcome by a feeling of nausea. A siren started to whine, an oddly effeminate, wavering wail of alarm somewhere on the roof; the physical proximity of the major became so nauseating that Herman, mumbling "People out there need help!" darted from under the desk and made for the door.

As he ran down the corridor, glass crunched under his feet. He caught glimpses of rooms behind lopsided doors; secretaries, cowering under desks, gazed at him with horrified eyes. Finally he found himself on the steps in front of the building. The drone of planes faded away in the distance and left an eerie stillness, until the buzzing of bees took up its somnolent hum once more. The white gravel of the drive, blinding in the sun, was gutted with craters in rings of dark soil, like giant black flowers. The cambodja trees stood naked and wintry without a blossom left on their branches. In front of the steps, exquisitely beautiful and vainglorious even in death, lay the peacock, its tail spread out on the gravel.

As Herman stood gazing at it, he heard in the distance the sound of thin, high screams and realized that indeed there must be wounded.

Behind him, a voice said, "My friend, I have misjudged you." He turned around; the major, gray with dust, eyelashes powdered, eyes madly elated, was standing in the doorway. "What you did was one of the bravest things I've ever seen a civilian do," he said. "Shake, sir."

Herman, who had no idea what the man was talking about, again felt he was taking part in a farce as they stood solemnly shaking hands amid the devastation.

"Well," the major said, with insane cheeriness, "let's go and tackle this mess! It always looks worse than it is."

3   The nuns of the Sacred Heart Educational Mission, thirty miles inland in the jungle, saw the planes come over and heard the distant thunder of bombs. A fearful silence fell over the small settlement of dormitories and palmetto roofs on stilts that served as classrooms. Everyone went about their business, even the native amahs, but many felt sick with fright.

Not so Sister Ursula, elderly nun in charge of the retarded children. She paid no attention, for little Saïdja was almost, almost there. After five months of patient coaching and fervent praying on her part he was almost able to finish lacing the shoe alone. The shoe was a wonderful educational aid. God's ways were mysterious indeed, if you considered how anything so simple and homely as an old boot could serve to guide a desperately retarded Dyak child from animal terror up the first steps toward humanity. In the beginning, Saïdja had been incapable of coordinating any movement that was not directed at his mouth; for days on end he had sat in a corner, drooling, steeped

17

in idiocy, gnawing on that shoe until a corner of it had gone quite soft. Merely to get him interested in lacing it was a triumph, the first spark of awareness in what had seemed until that moment a mere vegetable, for even an animal of that age was more capable of play than this poor little mite sitting there gnawing on a shoe. Once he had started putting the lace through the two bottom holes, the spark had caught and in the primeval darkness where his mind lay hibernating a first awareness had started to glow. It had been like watching God create man all over again, from the earliest beginnings, when there was nothing in the universe but wind and darkness. By some mysterious revelation from beyond the boundaries of his senses Saïdja had realized darkly that the ladder to consciousness, to humanity, to Christ, to God, ran up that shoe. It had taken weeks to keep his interest concentrated long enough for him to put the lace through the second pair of holes. There were eight in all, and Saïdja's lonely road from the first day of creation to the birth of Christ had seemed endless and fraught with danger and frustration. Sister Ursula had doubted whether he would ever make it; but that morning, just as the messenger came stumbling into the compound, Saïdja had made it. After that, nothing else seemed of much importance that day, whatever the message might be that the native runner had brought with such dramatic urgency.

At the noonday meal, when the nuns were seated at the long refectory table in the dining room with Father Sebastian at the head and the Reverend Mother at the far end, Father broke the news. The Japanese had landed in British Borneo and Rauwatta had been attacked from the air; the island was a theater of war now, despite their hopes and prayers. He said it calmly and with great composure; after a brief, queasy feeling of panic, Sister Ursula relaxed in total confidence that Father Sebastian could be trusted to find a practical solution that would benefit them all.

"Does this mean we'll have to evacuate?" Sister Synforosa asked.

Father Sebastian replied that he had given the matter some thought and decided that the best thing for them to do was to stay put, at least for the moment, and await instructions from the military. To start off on their own, now that war was a fact, would be foolhardy. "In the meantime, however, we should prepare for any eventuality," he added calmly.

There was a short silence around the table as the full meaning of those words penetrated to them.

"But we will be able to evacuate the children, won't we?" Sister Catharine asked anxiously.

Father Sebastian looked at his hands and weighed his words before he spoke. "We'll have to consider this from all angles," he said finally. "I think it would be premature for me to voice a definite opinion. For the time being we should all fervently pray that it will not be necessary."

"We certainly won't be able to evacuate *all* the children," said Sister Anna, a practical girl who was in charge of the household under the Reverend Mother.

Sister Ursula frowned. "Why not?"

"Well, there are one hundred and thirteen of them, including yours. Can you see us shepherding a hundred and thirteen children through the jungle to—" Anna looked at Father Sebastian. "Yes, where would we be taking them?"

"I cannot say anything at this juncture," Father Sebastian replied. "Let's cross that bridge when we get to it." He looked blandly at Sister Ursula and gave her the ghost of a smile. At that moment she knew that he had crossed the bridge already. Whatever happened to the other children, he was going to leave her thirteen retarded ones behind. At the same moment she knew, with an irrevocability that contracted her stomach, that she could not possibly leave Saïdja and the others to their fate.

From then on it seemed as if she were an outsider, listening with no more than casual interest to the talk around the table, treacherous talk which served only to prepare a justification for

19

deserting the children. It seemed as if she knew all the arguments before they were spoken. But one thing no one could argue away: their task was to represent Christ in this jungle. Whatever their rational apprehensions might be, they must at all times ask themselves what Jesus would have done under the circumstances. As to that there could be no doubt: He would rather go through the crucifixion all over again, with all its torment and pain and desperation, than desert His little flock of helpless lambs and abandon them to the wolves.

Sister Ursula was overcome with anger at the mere thought, a fury so sinful that she closed her eyes and prayed for deliverance from this visitation. Her prayer was answered at once; the moment she turned within herself and concentrated on her calling, it left no room for the judgment of others.

As she sat listening to the Sisters preparing their case for the desertion of those in their care, she knew that she would not only stay behind but be proud to do so. It was as if Christ had singled her out for a glorious mission of love.

4   The war caught the legendary Captain Krasser and his coaster *Henny* unawares, in the port of Tarakan.

The *Henny* carried freight and passengers along the west coast of Borneo, serving harbors that were too shoaled or unprofitable for the Royal Dutch Packet ships. She was probably the only seagoing vessel in the world commanded by a midget: Captain Krasser was just over four feet tall, with a man's head and torso but the arms and legs of a sturdy toddler. His deformity would have precluded a nautical career anywhere except in the Dutch East Indies. The huge colony on the equator, rhapsodized by hack poets as "an emerald girdle studded with jewels," had been conquered by Dutch privateers in the seventeenth century; their descendants still cherished a tradition of raffish derring-do and panache of which a midget captain on a captured freighter was considered to be a personification.

Captain Krasser was outrageously antisocial, an aggressive atheist who lost no opportunity to taunt the clergy and scandalize the prudish. He kept a harem of two Dyak tarts on board; lipstick marked his charts and black hairs were said to mess up his navigation by blurring his sextant. He had the reputation of parading his whores in front of priests among his passengers, and of dancing himself—naked, with horns—in front of missionaries when in his cups. He trained the ship's dogs, of whom he had had a succession, to be atheists also: they would refuse cookies if announced as coming from a priest and snap them up if from an atheist. He had written outrageous letters to the editors of all Far East newspapers, could not be received in the company of ladies and was dangerous when drunk; yet he was one of the most beloved eccentrics of the Archipelago. The Dutch East Indies were an empire, and emperors needed jesters, traditionally allowed to break all rules and insult the mighty. Although staunchly Calvinist, the Dutch colonials were tolerant and even understanding in the face of his virulent atheism, as a man cursed with his deformity was justified in being angry with God.

His ship, the *Henny,* was famous in her own right, and not only for the fact that she had a narrow platform running the length of her bridge to enable her captain to look over the sprayshield. Krasser had acquired her at the end of the First World War, when the defeated Germans were forced to give up their small slice of the emerald girdle studded with jewels. She had been old-fashioned even then, but her price was exceptionally low. There were rumors that Captain Krasser had paid nothing at all, but seized her with a crew of Chinese pirates the moment the Germans abandoned her at the dock in Celebes. He sailed her to Borneo, and there he shortened her name from *Grossherzogin Henrietta Cäcilie* to *Henny* because, as every sailor knows, to change a ship's name brings bad luck. She was an ungainly vessel with a thin, raking funnel which vainly tried to give some raciness to her lines; she was eminently suited, however, for her new task of crawling up unnavigable rivers, squeezing past uncharted banks at all times of the year, even when the wet monsoon changed the streams to torrents and colored the blue sea a murky brown for miles offshore. Her gross tonnage was 900, but, because of her broad beam, her draft only eight feet fully loaded. She could float where the haughty swans of the Royal Packet ran aground and her huge, slow, cast-iron propeller served as a woodchopper more than a screw when she nosed her way up the snag-tangled rivers of the swamps on the east coast. She had been known to churn her way through a newly born bank across the mouth of Boner River by backing into it with her cast-iron millstone and digging her way through. There was nothing, Captain Krasser boasted proudly, that the *Henny* would not do except fly.

The predicament in which the captain found himself this time was different. He had just finished unloading at the Beatrix Pier when bombs began to fall; after the planes left, the *Henny* was undamaged but the harbor a shambles. As he stood looking from the vantage point of the platform on his bridge at the burning oil tanks, the listing ships belching smoke, the greasy black pall that hung over the city, one thing was obvious: he had to get out of here, fast.

He was about to leave when an open convertible came racing down the dock and stopped alongside with squealing tires. Out jumped an Army officer and three native privates, armed to the teeth, accompanied by a white corporal. The officer cried, "Stop! Hold fast there!" and ran up the gangway to the deck. Captain Krasser gestured to his Chinese sailors, who had been about to cast off the *Henny*'s moorings, and waddled to meet the officer in a black mood of defiance.

"Take me to your captain," the officer snapped as they collided at the bottom of the stairs to the bridge.

"I am the captain."

The officer's face, despite the calamity the town had just suffered, went through the standard expressions of a healthy man in the vigor of youth confronting a midget. "Oh—er—well, I want a word with you in your quarters."

"Talk here. I'm leaving."

The officer frowned. His face was smeared with coagulated blood from a cut on his forehead. "You'll do nothing of the sort," he replied. "Your ship has been requisitioned by the Army for evacuation purposes. Corporal!" The white NCO leaped to attention behind him, gun in hand. "Post your men at the bollards and see to it that this ship stays were it is."

"On whose authority?"

"Look around you," the officer replied. "Maybe that will give you some idea. Your passengers will arrive shortly." He turned to leave.

"How many?" the captain asked. "And what am I supposed to do with them?"

"As many as you can hold. And you'll receive your orders."

"But I have no provisions!"

"Over there," the officer said, pointing at a burning warehouse. "Take as much as you can salvage. But better be nippy about it, it's one hell of a fish-fry." He turned around, strode down the gangway, climbed into his convertible, backed, turned and raced off, tires screeching. The native soldiers took up the key positions allotted to them; each of them carried a rifle with bayonet, a pistol and a bunch of hand grenades. No wonder they had a lot of self-confidence.

Krasser watched until the convertible had rounded the corner at the far end of the Beatrix Pier, then called his Chinese bo'sun, ordered him to take as many men as he could muster and start hauling provisions out of the burning warehouse. He waddled to his chartroom, where he found Kwan Chan waiting for him; a chart of Tarakan harbor lay ready on the table; compasses, parallel rulers, a pencil and a mug of coffee were lined up, and a stool for the Master to stand on. The boy was turning into a perfect mate, too perfect for comfort; when Krasser saw

24

the young Chinese standing there, smiling, after anticipating all his wishes with such radiant servility, he realized once again that the illiterate adolescent he had liberated from a brothel in Pontianak had become obsessed with a dream: a ship of his own. And guess whose ship he had in mind.

Krasser climbed onto the tabouret and looked at the chart. To break out of Tarakan harbor against the Army's orders was insubordination; to knock out a corporal and three privates, as he would have to do in order to get away, would make it mutiny. And that would present young Chinese angel-face with the perfect setup: the *Henny* at sea, after disobeying the Army's orders and dumping four of the Queen's soldiers over the side. It would be the ideal moment for the boy to get rid of him, take over the ship, bring her back to port and claim he had recaptured her for the Army from her delinquent captain. Kwan Chan had certainly come a long way from the cowed, timorous adolescent he had adopted. He knew he had given the impression of late of becoming an old man, full of nostalgia and childhood memories. Well, he'd show the little bastard a thing or two.

"There, Kwan Chan," he said in a tone of guileless excitement. "Have a look at the chart. To sneak out of here by the new channel would be asking for trouble; chances are that cannon have been put on the pierheads to blast away at the Japanese when they come. So if we want to sneak out under the cover of darkness we'll have to use the old channel, which is badly shoaled. It's new moon, all buoys will be extinguished as well as the lighthouse; nobody will see us ghost by. Even if they do, they won't suspect what we're up to, as the old channel was closed to shipping before the time of the youngsters now in control of the city. Only that smart-aleck pilot Bastiaans may guess our intention, but if Bastiaans isn't dead by now he must be snafued in some conference with the Army or the Navy. Those boys gather for conferences like game at a watering hole, even while the tigers are prowling. Yes—the old channel is our only chance. It will be high water at eleven, we'll leave at midnight."

The young Chinese raised his eyebrows. "Midnight? But you said high tide is at eleven, *tuan?*"

"That's right."

"Will we not be too late at the bar?"

Krasser smiled. The boy had really turned out smart; might have been his son. He deliberated whether he would dig another spadeful of his own grave by telling him why they would leave so late. But he felt in a generous mood, so he added, "The bar must be a real roadblock by now. If we want to get through we'll have to back our way through. In that case it's better to have the outgoing current than a couple of inches of higher water at slack tide. Understand?"

The boy nodded. There was a fleck of light in his dark eyes. God, he was keen. But Kwan Chan was not important at this moment. "Let's have a look at thirty-one," Krasser said.

Kwan Chan brought out the medium chart of the coastal waters below Tarakan. The nearest hiding place after leaving the harbor would be the mouth of Karimaka River; but it was too open, and alive with Dyak fishermen, some of whom must be Japanese spies. The only place to hide in safety was the turning basin off the mouth of Saraka River, a spot so remote and eerie that even the Dyaks rarely went there. Often in the past he had used the little cove to clean the waterline of his ship and pick up some free coal. It was a small natural harbor, surrounded by dead trees bleached white by the sun, known to the natives as the Pond of the Dead because there the separation of fresh and salt water occurred, and the drowned from upriver rose to the surface as they entered the salt water. The free coal was provided by a dump, overgrown beyond recognition, which he himself had thrown there twenty years ago for the use of the steam barge of an oil company surveying the river. The survey had proved unsuccessful, the coal was left where it was and he had only occasionally nibbled at it, keeping the bulk of it for an emergency. It must have been second sight.

"What about the soldiers, *tuan?*" Kwan Chan asked with a sweet smile.

"I'll leave them to you, boy."

The smile remained unchanged. "Very well, *tuan.*" It must be a blow to the young bastard, who obviously had hoped that Krasser himself would bash their skulls in.

"Only, don't hurt 'em, boy."

"Ah?"

"Disarm them, put them in the raft once we're at sea and set them adrift."

"Very well, *tuan.*"

It was good to know that the Chinese boy had no inkling of his reason for not harming the soldiers. "That'll be all," he said. "Tell the engine room to stand by."

"Very well, *tuan.*"

After the boy had left, Krasser stood gazing at the chart. The Pond of the Dead. Yes, that would be the spot. This was not his war, he wanted no part of it. Dutch, Japanese, Germans, English, Americans, they were all the same to him; let them fight it out among themselves. His country was called *Henny,* he was its king, and it was neutral, like Switzerland.

How long would Switzerland be able to stay neutral and ignore the war? He did not assume for a moment, as the military and the Navy seemed to be doing, that the Dutch would be able to stem the tide. The Japanese Navy would be here soon, the Strait of Macassar would be under constant surveillance. If he wanted to go on to Java he should not hang around. For the next few weeks it would be a real mess out there, and it was easier to slip by unnoticed while the dogs were fighting among themselves than after one of them had been victorious. But it was crazy to sail an old, slow coaster across the open sea while two giant navies were at war, sinking every vessel in sight. The sensible thing would be to stay in the Pond of the Dead, camouflage his ship with palms and mangroves to prevent her being spotted from the air and sit out the war. He could live for many months on the stores he carried. His Chinese crew would stay put, for they knew what their fate would be at the hands of the Japanese. The two Dyak tarts would certainly not mind, it would finally give them the chance to turn the chartroom into a parlor. He would catch up on his reading, go hunting and fishing, and maybe build a tree house, a boyish daydream he had never been able to realize. It was an attractive prospect, but first he had to get out of this harbor unnoticed. It would take one hell of a sailor to perform that feat. Well, whatever his other problems were, he had no worry on that score. It would be one more tall tale to make the rounds of the clubs, or, as was more likely now, the prison camps.

He poured himself a drink, tossed it back in one gulp. He smacked his lips, wiped his mouth with the back of his hand and looked at the chart again. The Pond of the Dead. That's where he'd take good old *Henny*.

He poured himself another drink and wondered where the girls were. There would be time for a quick roll in the hay before leaving. But he decided against it. First things first. That bar would be a hard nut to crack. Better take a nap while he had the chance.

A couple of hours later there was a knock on his door. It was his Chinese bo'sun, with the information that the provisions they had salvaged from the burning warehouse at the risk of their lives turned out to be dogfood. He held out a sample: a can labeled *Fido's Delight, two parts chicken gizzards to one part beef hearts. The treat wise puppies bark for.*

Krasser shrugged. He didn't care one way or another. What was good enough for a dog was good enough for a Chinese.

5   The havoc wrought in the town of Rauwatta by the air raid was a great deal worse than it had looked from the steps of Government House. Herman Winsum, the major and a dazed Eurasian lieutenant called Hin went into town to survey the damage, using the major's car, which had miraculously escaped destruction.

There were many fires; all streets within a radius of a mile from the road to the river turned out to be strewn with debris and pitted with bomb craters. They soon had to get out and walk. From mounds of smoking rubble in the moonscape of splintered trees and defoliated shrubs came the wails of the buried; for the first few minutes Herman felt he was going to be useless. He had never been able to stand the sight of blood; sick relatives he had been forced to visit in the past had always filled him with a faint revulsion he had been unable to overcome, despite frantic familial dedication. The wanton massacre he was now facing filled every fiber of his body with one urge: flight.

What kept him from turning around and running away was the presence of the Eurasian lieutenant. The delicate-looking young officer waded straight into the shambles of the first bungalow they came across and started to pull away beams and splintered doors to get at the source of a voice pleading nightmarishly in its tomb. The major made off, crying, "I'll get an ambulance!"

Herman was tempted to call out, 'I'll be back as soon as I can!' but the lieutenant's single-minded dedication to his neighbor wailing in his tomb presented a challenge. After a moment's hesitation, Herman joined the young man and started to heave away beams and fling aside shutters himself. When they dragged the first wounded out of the debris he felt a wave of nausea, closed his eyes and had the extraordinary sensation of having his face slapped. He opened his eyes, startled; it was the lieutenant, who had taken his closing his eyes as the beginning of a faint. From that moment on he no longer minded the blood. On the contrary, the despair, the pointless, tearful hope with which people clung to him after having been dragged from their graves gave him a feeling of strength that had grown into a sense of power by the time Mrs. Bohm arrived on the scene.

She emerged as Head of Volunteer Nurses. She looked clean, composed and utterly in control. She was wearing white overalls and a sun hat and carried a clipboard with a legal pad. While her underlings, eyes wide with horror, started to look after the wounded and carry them to the waiting ambulance on stretchers, Mrs. Bohm noted their names and addresses on her legal pad and also on strips of adhesive tape which she attached to their wrists. She handled the situation so efficiently that Herman realized she was actually enjoying herself; for some reason he was suddenly overcome with a wave of disturbingly joyful lust. There she was, tower of strength, full of vitality and purpose; he found himself reflecting what it would be like to throw her on her back, once all this was over, wash the blood off her body, towel her skin to tingling life and sink with her into soul-shattering debauchery. He trusted that whoever saw him work among the wounded, the dead and the dazed would not suspect that the Good Samaritan was preoccupied with the prospect of fornication.

When they had taken five more people out of another mound of smoking rubble, two of them so mangled that identification was impossible, he stood at the foot of this Golgotha, looked across at Mrs. Bohm and sent her a silent message. But before she had time to receive it, the effeminate siren on the roof of Government House squealed its genteel wail of panic again.

They barely had time to duck for shelter before bombs came shrieking down once more; when it was over, the Eurasian lieutenant lay quite still a few feet away in the basement in which Herman found himself. The man looked as frail as a girl in his uniform designed for Dutch farmers and quite dead. When the All Clear sounded Herman shook him by the shoulders, crying, "Lieutenant! Lieutenant! Are you all right?" The young man sat up, looked about him and after a moment of disorientation got back to his feet.

Together they staggered out into the open and found to their surprise that, although this second bombardment had seemed worse than the first, there was no new damage, in their part of town at least. There were fires in the native district, however, which the previous attack had spared. Major Benstra turned up in his car, which was still running, though on flapping tires. "There's trouble in the kampong!" he cried. "I'm off to take a look. Hin, and you too, Winsum, start organizing the evacuation. Women, children and wounded by plane, men on foot!" With that, he snorted off in his plopping vehicle, last of the Keystone Kops.

Herman and the lieutenant looked at one another for a moment, speechless; then, united in a sudden boyish conspiracy, they laughed. "Start the evacuation," Herman said. "Why me? I wouldn't know where to begin. Would you?"

It seemed as if he had touched the lieutenant in a sensitive spot, for the young man stiffened and answered curtly, "Of course."

"Look," Herman said, "I don't want to interfere, I know it's supposed to be your profession, but I happen to know the very person to help you organize the evacuation of the women, the children and the wounded: Mrs. Bohm, the woman who was here when this second attack started."

Hin said, "All right. Would you contact her?"

"With pleasure. You know where you can round up some planes?"

"There were only a few Piper Cubs on the airfield," the lieutenant replied.

"Won't your headquarters be sending us planes? Surely they know we have been under air attack twice today?"

"My sergeant is supposed to have kept up radio contact. I'll go and investigate."

"All right—let's meet in Government House a couple of hours from now," Herman said.

"Er—very well," the lieutenant said, still unsure as to how to handle their relationship.

"Let's hope we'll soon be able to relax somewhere and have a meal together."

The lieutenant saluted and said stiffly, "The name is Hin." Then he turned away and marched off.

As Herman leap-frogged over piles of rubble he reflected how odd it was, this short interplay of formality in the midst of disaster. There was no formality about Mrs. Bohm when he finally tracked her down in the major's office in Government House. The mousy woman who had played the part of Gwendolen in *The Importance of Being Earnest* the night before sat at a little table outside the office door, wearing a nurse's cap which Mrs. Bohm must have looted from the hospital.

Herman asked, "Is she in there?"

Gwendolen, obviously reliving a secretarial past, said, "One moment, please." She went inside, came back and said, "Mrs. Bohm will see you now."

"Thank you." He went in.

It was interesting to see Mrs. Bohm's reaction to his emerging in the middle of her organizing everybody in sight. She sat writing at the major's desk as he came in, and the first glance she shot him was hostile. Then her frown relaxed, her Delft-blue eyes became placid again with that diffused gaze of sensuality he had come to recognize and she said, "Hello, stranger. What can I do for you?"

He repressed the obvious answer. "A mess, isn't it?"

She looked at him with a hint of steel in her eyes. "Oh," she said, "I've seen worse."

"Where?"

"Shanghai, '37. We had a whole month of this."

"Must be odd to go through it for a second time."

"No," she said. "It's odder the first time. How is your end doing?"

He smiled at her and felt it turn into a lewd grin. "The major has ordered me and the lieutenant to organize the evacuation of the town."

"Evacuation to where?"

"That he didn't say. All he said was that the women, the children and the wounded should go by plane and the men on foot."

Instead of bursting into laughter as he had expected, she said, "That makes sense."

"Well, I'm glad you think so. Think you can handle the evacuation of the women, the children and the wounded?"

"Certainly. When are we expected at the airfield?"

He wasn't sure whether she was bluffing. "Lieutenant Hin is trying to establish contact with his headquarters. I may be able to tell you in an hour or so."

"Good enough." She turned back to whatever she had been writing when he came in.

"Could you, please, tell me how to go about organizing the evacuation of the men on foot?"

"Where are you supposed to go from here, sweetie?"

"I haven't the foggiest idea, darling."

"That's what I thought." Her smile was so relaxed that it drugged him into a state of happy unconcern. She really was a splendid woman. Her competence was such that he felt like sitting down, putting his feet on her desk and picking up a newspaper while she worked it out for him.

"Get hold of Sam Hendriks," she said. "He's your man. I tried to locate him, but I couldn't."

Herman frowned. Sam Hendriks had played the part of Lane, the butler, with a continuous leer. Not a presence to inspire confidence in a life-or-death situation. "Who is this Hendriks?"

"Oh, Sam runs a small plantation of Areca palms and coffee shrubs in the foothills. The coffee is a pretext; his Areca palms are used to make the local hooch and must be responsible for ninety percent of the drunks in this part of Borneo, including Sam Hendriks himself."

"Then why him?"

"Because he's been kicking around these hills for so long that he's likely to know the way."

"Where?"

"To the coast, where you can be picked up by ship."

"But why on foot? Why can't we just take whatever cars are left and drive to the coast?"

"The road has been bombed, and the major was going to

blow up the bridge," she said. "But maybe he hasn't yet. Let's find out."

She picked up the telephone, and was irritated to find it dead. She must be having a high old time, sitting there impersonating Florence Nightingale. She tapped the hook of the telephone impatiently, then put back the receiver and said coolly, "Why don't you and I organize our own evacuation?"

He gulped. God, she was unpredictable. What a fascinating woman. "That's what we set out to do, before the Japs hit the fan."

"Why occupy ourselves with these headless chickens?" She gazed at him dreamily. "Let them look after themselves while we make off into the mountains, just the two of us."

He thought for a moment that she meant it; then he realized it was merely pique on her part at being thwarted in her role of the Lady with the Lamp. He suddenly was sick of acting as her sidekick. He stood up and realized how tired he was; his whole body ached. Despite his sudden age of sixty, he bent over the desk and kissed her. Her lips were warm and responsive.

"Go and find Sam Hendriks," she whispered, as if she were organizing an orgy.

He straightened up and tried to stride out of her lair rather than stagger. Outside, in the corridor, in a smell of rubble dust and ether, Gwendolen, living her own secret playlet, was lighting emergency oil lamps in broad daylight.

The major and he met in the driveway. "This time they've bombed the road to Rokul," the major said briskly. "It runs through the kampong, there are many casualties. On top of everything else, a gang of prisoners working on the road escaped during the attack; there's been looting and murder. When the headhunters come down from the mountains, as they are sure to do, this place will turn into a nightmare. How far have you got with the evacuation?"

Lieutenant Hin joined them, stark white with rubble dust,

looking like a Papuan mud-dancer. He told the major he had contacted Banjermasin on the emergency transmitter. Headquarters would send three planes in the morning; Mrs. Bohm was organizing the women, the children and the wounded.

"What about the able-bodied men, Winsum?"

"I'm on my way to Sam Hendriks. He's been appointed to lead that part of the evacuation."

"Who in hell thought that one up?" the major asked derisively.

"Oh—er—Mrs. Bohm."

"She's out of her mind! All you need is a megalomaniac with delirium tremens to take you straight over the edge! No. Just round up the men; order them to bring rations for a week and to report at the airport tomorrow at noon, I'll take it from there. But hurry up! The fact that the Japs have bombed the road indicates that they have plans for Rauwatta. They may start parachuting troops any time. We blew up the bridge, but they may parachute rafts for the crossing. Let's get out of here while the going is good!"

"Yes, sir," Herman said, saluting. The French bedroom farce had changed into *Journey's End*.

6　　The preparations for the evacuation of Rauwatta took all night. Herman, with implicit trust in Mrs. Bohm's judgment, managed to track down Sam Hendriks, despite the major's high-handed dismissal of the man as a viable guide. He found the planter at the bar in the Sports Circle, where, over a glass of whiskey, he was telling the native barman how to gut and roast a primate. Hendriks took the news of his assignment in his stride; he simply mumbled, "Tally-ho," finished his whiskey and ordered another.

Herman spent the rest of the night among the wounded who had been channeled by Lieutenant Hin to the passenger terminal at the airport, which, for reasons known only to the Japanese, had not been bombed. He did not see Mrs. Bohm again until the next morning, when she arrived at the airport shepherding a herd of mothers and children. Both she and the major were at the peak of their power; the major bellowed commands at the bedraggled recruits manning the anti-aircraft guns; Mrs.

Bohm soothed the panic of distraught mothers and the tantrums of terrified children by her mere presence, immaculately dressed in white, carrying her clipboard, making notes that must be completely symbolical but suggested order, calm and efficiency. She joined Herman after a while, took him aside and said with uncharacteristic urgency, "Manny, you'd better leave with us, by air." Seen from close quarters, the woman who had sat behind the major's desk was different from the one who now stood amidst the shambles of white matronhood in Rauwatta. She had dark shadows under her eyes and the glint of steel had gone; in its stead there was a hint of despair. With a shock Herman realized that he was witnessing the disintegration of an empire. If Mrs. Bohm lost hope, the war was lost and there was nothing left for the white man but to flee.

"Why?" he asked.

"Don't join that hike across the mountains."

"What—what makes you say that?"

"All you men except Sam are city creatures. You won't last a day in those mountains, not as an organized group. After that it will be every one for himself, and none of you will make it."

"Come, come," he said, with a quiver in the pit of his stomach. "Don't be gloomy."

"Have you ever trekked through the jungle? Have you ever *been* in those mountains? Do you know what they're like?"

All he knew of the jungle and the mountains was what he had seen from the plane: a featureless broccoli field. The quiver in his stomach spread to his knees. "Don't worry," he said, "we'll make out."

"I'm not just trying to save your neck. I need you with the children and the wounded. You're a sensitive, delicate man, not a mountain climber. Your place is with the victims." It was nicely put, but her meaning was clear: not a man, but a child who needed protection.

38

"Thank you," he said, "but my place is with the men." He walked away, sick of her running his life for him.

He did not see her again until she came back with the major in his car after a last-minute round-up of stragglers. She came straight for him, ignoring Lieutenant Hin; the look she gave him was upsetting. It was unfocused, as if she were drunk. "Here," she said, holding out a stick and a booklet. "Take these."

"But—" He was interrupted by the major, who barked at the lieutenant, "Hin, take two men and leave for the Sacred Heart Mission at once! Escort the nuns downriver to Bunugawa, wait there for orders. Mrs. Bohm! Let's see what we've got here."

The major made off with her, leaving Herman and the lieutenant gazing at one another, Herman with an alpenstock and a brochure, Lieutenant Hin with an order to evacuate nuns. The book was called *The Edible Wild Plants of the Malay Archipelago.* The stick was hickory with a leather thong through the top. In it was carved: *Hit's curious all a body see, a-walking by his lone, outlandish birds and beasties' prints and traces in a stone.*

There was a sudden drone of planes. The siren on the roof of a hangar started wailing. The major shouted, "Take cover! Take cover!" Running toward a gun emplacement, he screamed, "Fire! Fire! Stupid apes, can't you see what's coming?" The gun started to stutter, hesitant at first, then with a vicious staccato, drowning the major's screams, "Stop! Stop! They're ours!"

They were indeed: two fighter planes, obviously sent as cover for the transport planes now appearing on the horizon behind them. The fighter planes banked sharply, engines snarling; the major stood shaking his fists at the gun crew in a pathetic display of powerless bungling. Then the fighter planes came back for a low pass.

Herman knew what they were going to do before it happened. They must have concluded that the airport was now occupied by the Japanese, for they came in, machine guns blazing, to strafe the runway. The major, with brainless heroism, rushed out into the open with a bedsheet off one of the stretchers, waving it as a white flag. He was killed on the spot. Herman never knew how he, the lieutenant and Mrs. Bohm managed to get the panicking herd of women and children under cover.

The major's sacrifice must have served some purpose, for the transport planes landed. The evacuees were crammed into them in sickening, horrifying numbers. When they took off it was obvious they were overloaded: they hopped lugubriously down the runway, like vultures that had gorged themselves. They barely made it over the hangar at the far end.

Herman listened to their engines with his eyes closed, incapable of watching what seemed to be inevitable disaster. But they made it, circled in a wide, laboring sweep, then droned away over the jungle. He had the sudden premonition that he would never see Mrs. Bohm again.

He himself was now headed for the jungle, part of a crowd of pampered white males who had occupied desks in a clearing in the wilderness called Rauwatta. While the men stood about undecidedly, each of them tasting the bile of fear in his own secret moment of truth, Sam Hendriks came cycling down the road, got off, put his bike against the wall of the gutted terminal building and asked, "Well? Where's everybody? Let's get this show on the road." He seemed cold sober, and Herman realized at those first words that God, in His infinite mercy, had sent them in their hour of need a male Mrs. Bohm.

With relaxed authority Sam Hendriks prepared the men for a hike through the mountains. He told them what shoes to take, what clothes, what headgear and to take as many lumps of sugar as they could stow away in their pockets. He ordered Mr. Palstra the pharmacist to bring along a small bottle of mint alcohol for each man.

When they finally reassembled by the ruins of the demolished bridge, Sam Hendriks explained the journey ahead. The first part would be the toughest: they would have to make a forced march to the mountains. Once there, they would move only by night to avoid being spotted from the air. He had with him an old Dyak guide who stood nodding by his side as he spoke. The Dyak was called Arula, and Sam said he was the best goddam jungle guide in Borneo, so there was no chance of their getting lost. As long as they were sensible, did not take more than one lump of sugar with one drop of mint alcohol at a time, they would all reach the coast unharmed and in reasonable comfort. "So, let's get going! Parson, how about getting God in on this? Give us a prayer for the road, there's a good chap."

An overweight middle-aged man started to intone a prayer at the top of his voice. He did not evoke the presence of God; he evoked echoes of a prehistoric past: medicine man to a small, lost tribe. Then they started to march.

They were barely out of town and among the plantations when other planes arrived, dropping big multicolored flowers over the airport and near the river. They were Japanese; the little black seeds dangling from the flowers were parachutists, the large yellow ones rubber rafts. Rauwatta had fallen.

7   When Sister Ursula saw a launch with an officer and two native soldiers arrive at the dock, she knew why they had come. She had been expecting them, everybody had. So far, Father Sebastian had been unable to bring himself to say anything about evacuation, he obviously had decided to wait for someone else to tell them. Well, here came that someone.

Father Sebastian went to meet the officer on the dock; then they closeted themselves in his office. The two soldiers, tired and hungry, were given a hearty breakfast by Sister Anna. When finally Father Sebastian and the officer emerged from their seclusion, Father rang the bell on the veranda; the nuns and the amahs gathered in the clearing to hear what he had to say. His message was simple: they had been ordered to evacuate the mission by "Caesar," as Father Sebastian called the shy, bewildered little Eurasian lieutenant with his two weary native soldiers. Nothing would have been easier for a determined man than to simply ignore whatever command the bedraggled trio had carried through the jungle, but Father Sebastian, barely able to hide his relief, built them up into an irresistible armed force which separated them with its overwhelming power from their Christian calling. When he finally announced that the children would remain behind, Sister Ursula cried involuntarily, "We ought to be ashamed of ourselves!"

It grieved Father Sebastian and enraged the Reverend Mother; it also woke up the little Eurasian officer, who had sat nodding by their side, losing his battle with exhaustion. "Come, Sister," Father Sebastian said in his most patient voice, "if you will just use your head rather than allow yourself to be overcome by the promptings of your generous heart, you will realize that, sad and upsetting as it may be, this is the only solution. It is a moot question whether we adults will safely reach the coast and find transportation to Java, or wherever else the Lord wants us to go. We cannot subject the children to the rigors of such an expedition. Also, most important, we should not incriminate them in the eyes of the Japanese invaders, who—"

"How could we possibly do that?" Sister Ursula asked, though she should have known better.

Father Sebastian raised a hand, closed his eyes with a pained expression and said, "Pray, Sister, let me finish! If there were the slightest doubt in my mind that our leaving the children behind might expose them to danger, I would agree with you. But the Japanese not only come with the slogan 'Asia for the Asians,' they also love children."

"Then what about staying here, instead of running for our lives?" Sister Ursula asked.

Reverend Mother snorted, Father Sebastian again closed his eyes and shook his head with paternal patience. "Sister, our presence would compromise our little ones as much as if we were to take them with us. Believe me, I have put this matter before God, and I have accepted the inevitability of this solution only after my own private night in the Garden of Gethsemane."

In the past, Sister Ursula had always been moved when Father Sebastian pointed out how Jesus' experiences were mirrored in the lives of every Christian, including his own; this time his claim to share in the suffering of Christ revolted her. "And what about *my* children?" she asked. "Will the Japanese love *my* children too?"

"Of course, of course," Father Sebastian said soothingly. "They love *all* children."

"Will they love mine sufficiently to keep the Dyaks from mistreating them after we have abandoned the mission?"

"Of course! The Japanese are civilized people. And Adinda will be staying to look after them. She looked after them before you came, I see no reason why she should be incapable of doing so again."

Sister Ursula tried to find words to tell him what she thought of that monstrous argument, considering the state the children had been in when she found them; but she was struck dumb. She stared at him as if he had ripped off a mask and revealed himself as a monster of selfishness and cowardice instead of the humble, devoted vicar of Christ she had admired so guilelessly. How could he stand there, looking holy and patient, and suggest that the children they had found tied to trees, crazed with fear, be thrown back into being no more than tethered animals, mouthing meaningless sounds, eating filth?

But after that flare-up of emotion she became very calm. She now would have to make her own plans. Father Sebastian, the Reverend Mother and her fellow Sisters would force her to go with them; to save the children she would have to be cunning, more cunning than she had ever been before in her life. If the others so much as suspected that she was planning to stay behind they would never let her out of their sight; she must pretend she had been convinced by Father Sebastian's argument or, if she could not bring that off, that she had decided to adhere to her vow of obedience. She would have to tell Adinda that she was going to leave, but there was no point telling the children, they would not understand. Also, they would sense the truth; had she decided in her heart to leave them, they would have known somehow and would now be deeply upset, crying and kicking and making desperate mischief the way they had the day she had gone to the coast with the launch because it was her turn to collect the mail and the stores from the coaster *Henny.*

Adinda believed her when she said, calmly and authoritatively, that she was leaving. Adinda did not seem to care; the unemotional, silent woman who had flowed into the mission with her starving charges of cretins and imbeciles like water following the way of least resistance would flow placidly and with utter passiveness back into the jungle after they left.

At first it seemed to Sister Ursula that she would be unable to put her plan into practice when the moment came. Forty years constituted a lifetime, and it proved unexpectedly hard to break a lifetime's habit of leaving her fate in the hands of her superiors. She went into the jungle to her private little chapel under the boughs of a waringin tree to pray for help, for guidance, not to her patron, St. Ursula, but directly to Christ. She begged for clearness, peace, openness to His will; the answer she received was so infinitely loving and soothing that she rose convinced her choice had been the right one.

A few hours before sunset Father Sebastian called all the nuns together in front of his bungalow, this time without the amahs and the native personnel. Lieutenant Hin had decided, he said, to get under way before dark, as there was a risk that rebels or Japanese might invade the Mission during the hours of darkness. He announced that the first boat would be commanded by Lieutenant Hin, the second by himself accompanied by the two soldiers. He proceeded to read a list of names and gave everybody her place in one of the boats; Sister Ursula was directed to the one under command of the lieutenant. Father

Sebastian finished by asking if everyone knew her place now, and they replied in unison, "Yes, Father."

"Very well, let us pray."

He prayed, his head tilted back, gazing at the sky, as was his wont. Sister Ursula had always been thrilled by his surrender to the Holy Spirit when he prayed; this time, as she listened to him imploring the heavenly Father to guide them and protect them and bless them with His mercy, she felt disgusted.

Father Sebastian's prayer was short; he obviously was in a hurry to get moving. Immediately after the Amen, he cried, "Sisters! Take your places! God be with us!"

The Sisters hastily picked up the bundles they had put down in order to fold their hands; the haste with which they scurried to the dock was shameful, but fortunate as it added an element of panic and confusion to the departure. When Sister Ursula told the lieutenant that she was joining Father Sebastian in his boat at his request instead of taking her allotted place in the first, the officer nodded absently, flustered by the sudden frenzy of his passengers.

She hurried back to the main building, supposedly on a last-minute errand. Inside the building she hid in the toilet. But as she sat there, listening to the distant sounds of departure, she suddenly became panic-stricken. Suppose someone came back at the last moment to use the bathroom. With all the nerves and the excitement it was quite likely. She became so certain that presently someone would rattle the doorknob and call, "Who's in there?" that she opened the door and slipped out.

There were sounds of activity in the distance, on the dock and the river's bank; the compound seemed deserted. It gave her an eerie feeling, she had not realized how empty the Mission would be after everyone had left. She ran, half crouching, along the outer edge of the clearing as fast as she could, down the winding jungle path to her hideout underneath the waringin.

She collapsed, panting, at the foot of the tree, and suddenly burst into tears.

She tried to tell herself not to be silly: this was not the moment to let herself go; if she felt like this, she should join the others at once. Of course there was no question of that, but she could not help herself. She scolded herself, she prayed, all to no avail; her sobs were stronger than her will. Then she heard the sound of engines starting up in the distance and slowly going away, downriver. She had no idea why, but it changed her from a sobbing bundle of silliness into a calm, composed mother on her way back to her children.

She returned to the edge of the compound and listened for sounds from the river, but there weren't any. Not a leaf stirred on its bank. From behind the matted screen of her open-air classroom she heard the bawling of her children. She wondered where the other children had gone, the native nurses, the amahs, the cooks. She was taken aback by their wholesale flight, it looked as if they had been waiting for this chance to slip back into the jungle.

When she opened the little screen door of the classroom she saw Adinda. The woman was sitting in the center of the clearing doing nothing, just sitting. The children crawled and waddled aimlessly around her, some whining, some bawling, some trying to get out; beside her lay little Saïdja's shoe. Sister Ursula looked for Saïdja himself and saw him squatting in a far corner, eating soil. He had not done that for months; the sight filled her with such resolve that from then on she never looked back.

"Adinda," she said, "I have taken over command until further notice. Go and round up the others. You and I are perfectly able to keep this Mission running efficiently until the Japanese commander turns up and tells us what we are to do." The woman looked at her impassively, understanding but not caring, then got heavily to her feet and slouched off. Maybe she would vanish, like the others.

"Saïdja!" Sister Ursula called, holding up the shoe. "Look what I've got!"

The little boy stared at her, mouth open; his chin was caked with mud. Then he gave a sound, a toneless sound of recognition that suddenly brought those silly tears back, and crawled toward her on all fours, bawling, "Sa-ja, Sa-ja," his name.

The other children came running, hopping and waddling toward her, threw themselves on her with a great show of emotion; she was smothered by eager little bodies crawling all over her like puppies searching for milk. She sensed, with a feeling of gratitude, that they were not upset at all; they merely wanted her to make a fuss of them.

That she did. She hugged them, kissed them, spoke endearments she did not usually indulge in. She had to be careful to whom she showed affection, she must split it into equal portions, for their overruling passion was jealousy. In the end they got so out of hand that she had to rally them back into some sort of order or there would have been real tears instead of just pretended ones. She said, "Children! Listen! We're going to sing! *The Lonely Ash Grove!*" In a strong, steady voice, she sang, *"In yonder green valley where streamlets meander, when twilight is falling, I pensively rove."*

They tried to faze her by pulling her hair, blowing into her ears, sticking their fingers in her mouth as she sang. But she kept at it, and when at last little Saïdja picked up his shoe and started to beat the ground with it as he bawled, she calmed him down. They all realized that her moment of indulgence was over and settled back happily into the fixed pattern of their rigorously identical days. The only thing they had to cling to on their stumbling way to humanity was the routine she had established; as long as neither she nor the routine faltered they would feel secure and loved and go on groping their way toward the light.

She sang *The Lonely Ash Grove* to its end, then *Flow Gently, Sweet Afton.* Her voice sounded strong until she became conscious of her loneliness in the silence of the empty compound. Nobody had come back; darkness was about to fall. But it was as if Christ stood behind her in calm, comforting assurance.

"Children," she said, "bedtime!" She got up, went to the screen door and opened it to let them out. Standing outside, in a long silent row, were all the women and the girls who had fled into the jungle. They gazed at her in awe, and for a second she felt an almost sinful triumph. But she rallied at once and said, "All right, everybody! Back to your posts! Nanja, go to your kitchen. Adinda, help me give the children a bath. Supper at six, and we'll have it together, in the dining room."

They turned away and set about their tasks, as relieved as the children had been when they saw her familiar white hair appear once more after, for a few bewildering hours, they had felt abandoned.

8   The coaster *Henny*'s escape from Tarakan harbor was surprisingly easy. The bar proved less shoaled than Captain Krasser had expected; everybody ashore was far too busy with martial games to notice the shadow ghosting down the disused channel and out into the open sea. Immediately outside the harbor the balsa-wood raft was tossed over the side and the trussed-up corporal and soldiers were lowered into it; then the *Henny,* still showing no lights and steaming at half-speed to muffle the sound of her wheezing old engine, headed for the coast.

But it soon became apparent that the rest of Krasser's plan had to be revised. There was a lot of traffic in the darkness; the danger of being spotted was greater than he had foreseen. So instead of heading straight for the Pond of the Dead as he had planned, he was forced to sneak into the nearest cove to camouflage his ship before going any farther.

It took two days; by the time the island *Henny* was ready to sail, Kwan Chan had created a masterpiece. Even from as close

50

as a couple of hundred yards it was difficult to recognize the cluster of palm trees, mangroves and jungle creepers as a ship. Kwan Chan had been enthusiastically assisted by the crew; the operation had appealed to a boyish element in them. Several of them had come up with ideas of their own; one had painted the white streaks of cormorant droppings on the dark leaves of the mangroves, another had built a bird's nest and stuck it on top of a palm tree at the risk of his neck. The result was a small tropical island, so realistic that butterflies settled in the trees.

The *Henny* left the cove at nightfall. As she slowly moved into the open, the tropical night enveloped her in its starry splendor. A thin moon, floating on its back, drew a quivering trail across the oily sea. It was so tranquil that the night seemed hushed with awareness of the new little island bravely coursing out to sea. In the distance rumbled the intermittent thunder of gunfire; there must be a naval battle in progress, or maybe Japanese or Dutch gunners were just firing at ghosts. It was that kind of night.

Krasser stayed on the bridge while his island inched down the coast of Borneo. He ordered Kwan Chan to clear spaces in the foliage so he could see out. The old telephone line between the forecastle and the bridge was reactivated. Still he felt like a horse with blinkers; but after sailing this coast for thirty years he knew it like a milkman's nag its daily run, he virtually could find his way in his sleep.

The crew was so excited about the ship's transformation that the watch off duty stayed on deck. His two girls didn't sleep either; he could hear them giggle on the lower bridge and smelled the sweet aroma of their opium pipes. Occasionally he heard the call of the mynah bird: a wolf whistle, followed by *"I love yew"* directed at Fifi, the ship's dog, rummaging under the mangroves.

When the dark blue sky started to turn luminous with the dawn, Krasser was overcome by a feeling of unreality. It was as if his little island beneath the still, pure boat of the moon had detached itself not only from the shore but from the rest of mankind. But when they arrived in the mouth of the Ramoko River at daybreak and he dropped anchor inside the spit, he was back in reality. With it came exhaustion, and irritation at the two doped women sprawling naked in his bunk in wide-legged abandon. He stood for a moment staring at them and was about to start kicking drawers shut when he saw Fifi, the dog, roll over, ears back, licking her nose, lying in abject surrender. He knew that the animal took all loud noises as directed at her and would wet the floor if he so much as kicked one drawer. Of all those on board, only the worthless little mongrel possessed the secret of mollifying him; he bent down, scratched her belly, which was bristly and unattractive but to him utterly endearing, and growled, "All right, slut, cut it out." Fifi sprang to her feet relieved and took up her cookie stance: sitting on her haunches, front paws begging, ears cocked. Everyone in Borneo was familiar with this trick: the ship's dog refusing a biscuit when it came from "a priest" and snatching it when it was announced as coming from "an atheist"—it was one of the standard stories about Captain Krasser. There were others, most of them apocryphal, about his paranoid hatred of priests, all churches and all forms of religion; and the standard one of his dancing stark naked in front of three terrified schoolteachers of the Anglican Mission in Batung Baru with horns on his head, crying obscenities at the sky, daring God to prove His existence by striking him dead. No one knew the true origin of his anticlerical fury; rumor had it that he had been jeered at as a child in a Protestant orphanage because of his size until he broke free and set out on his piratical career.

The truth was more complex. His father, a blacksmith, had been an alcoholic bully who terrorized his wife and six children with bouts of drunken violence until they turned into cowed victims—all, that is, except his midget son. As a consequence, the beatings became aimed at the stunted child who refused to be reduced to a terrified rabbit. The abuse became so serious that the mother consulted their minister, a somber man with a grim belief in predestination, who had explained the child's deformity by quoting Exodus 20:5, *For I the Lord thy God am a jealous God, visiting the iniquity of the fathers upon the children.* He advised prayer, and also had a talk with the brute, who as a result flew into a murderous rage and nearly killed wife and runt. The next day young Krasser waddled off to freedom and stowed away in the cable hold of an ocean-going tugboat bound for China. What made him break away and set out on his own was not the violence of his demented father. It was the concept that his deformity was someone else's punishment. The thought that he had been crippled at birth as God's retribution for his father's behavior set him off on his lifelong crusade: to unmask the hypocrites who peddled this obscene concept, to unmask all religion as superstition and to prove, whenever he saw the chance, that God did not exist but was an invention of the clergy. It was an irony of fate that the very origin of his atheism, his droll size, turned out to be the worst enemy of his cause; to the planters, businessmen and minor government officials who frequented the clubs of the Dutch East Indies, the midget and his crusade of enlightenment became a constant source of merriment. He knew this, and in time was slowly overcome by the mute rage of powerlessness. His courageous atheism, the bold challenge of his acts of moral rebellion like living with two whores and burying the dead at sea with no more than the callous command *"Ajo lekas!"*—'hurry up!'—became, instead of a witness of his faith, the stuff barroom anecdotes were made of. By the time the *Henny* fled from the burning port of Tarakan, the only one who took Captain Krasser's atheism seriously was Fifi.

This morning, however, he felt weary of the cookie ritual; he poured himself a drink and gave Fifi her dog biscuit without the usual routine. That upset her thoroughly. When he failed to put it on her snout, telling her it came from a priest, she rolled onto her back and started to lick her nose again.

"All right!" he growled. "From an atheist! Take it!"

Fifi accepted the cookie as if she were doing him a favor.

"Cut it out," Krasser said. "You're a dog, not a woman."

As she lay crunching her biscuit at his feet, he heard over the sharp crackling of her chewing a chorus of shouts in the distance. He was on his way to the door when Kwan Chan appeared. *"Tuan!"* he cried. *"Tuan!* Look!" He pointed at the shore.

Krasser hoisted himself onto the platform on the bridge and looked. On the small beach of the cove stood or knelt a small crowd of people; their hails, shouts and chanted prayers rang out across the water. They must be refugees from the interior.

The last thing he needed at this point was passengers. They would upset his crew, devour his stores and make his spending the war in the Pond of the Dead impossible. He should leave at once; but it was broad daylight. Despite his camouflage, to venture out into the open after the gunfire he had heard overnight would be suicidal. There was nothing he could do except ignore them. Let them shout and wave and prance to their heart's content; he was going to bed.

Kwan Chan, standing beside him, was obviously waiting for orders, but the hell with him. The mynah bird in the mangroves gave its wolf whistle and crooned that it loved him as Krasser waddled to his cabin. There he stripped and was about to chase the two snoring women out of his bunk, but he chickened out; they would scream blue murder. Muttering under his breath, he went through the door to the messroom and climbed onto the leatherette seat, which instantly stuck to his perspiring skin as he lay down.

He was almost asleep when somebody came in, breathing heavily, obviously in a state of excitement. Krasser opened his eyes, peered over the tabletop and saw a clergyman in a torn, smudged white suit and dog-collar, unshaven, with the eyes of a lunatic. At the sight of the hairy dwarf rising from behind the table the man's eyes filled with tears and he cried in a voice hoarse with emotion, "Bless you! Bless you, angel of God! Bless you!"

"Who the hell are you?" Krasser asked.

"I'm Pastor Zandstra from Tjelok Barung! I have part of my congregation with me, ashore. Our town was attacked by planes; we walked for two days and three nights through the jungle; I can't tell you what we went through. My people lost heart, but I prayed and prayed. God, how I prayed! I assured them that we would be saved, that God would have mercy on us, and behold: He sent you!"

Krasser gaped at him as the man slumped into the chair opposite, dried his perspiring forehead and continued, "Now you and I will have to talk about the arrangements. I have twenty souls in all: seven men, six women, the rest children. What kind of accommodations do you have? Obviously we'll have to keep the women and the children separated from the men, where sleeping quarters are concerned. I also noticed that you have filled your decks with greenery; but I wonder if we couldn't clear a space for daily prayer services and perhaps make a quiet corner for the religious education of the little ones. Let me see, what else was there?" He frowned, thinking; he looked lucid and collected, but his hand on the table shook and there was something in his eyes that belied his composure. He must be as close to a nervous breakdown as a Javanese about to run *amok.* "Ah yes. We don't want to give you a lot of trouble, but I do think that in view of the present state of religious awareness of my flock we should have fish on Fridays. We must certainly banish all liquor." He stared at the captain with a smile that looked insane. "As a God-fearing man on an errand of mercy, I'm sure you'll agree with all this." He did not wait for Krasser's reaction, but plowed on. "Then perhaps we should radio our church headquarters in Batavia that, owing to God's mercy, I have been able to guide at least part of my congregation out of the wilderness. I'll give you the list of names. My own name is Zandstra: Reverend A. Now—"

The door to the cabin squeaked open and in came the two girls, naked but for skimpy sarongs. Amu carried a tray with two glasses and Baradja the earthenware crock of the captain's gin. The clergyman's mouth fell open.

Krasser asked, "Glass of rotgut, Reverend?"

The Reverend gulped. The girls, who always perked up at the sight of a new man on board, planned to stay, but after they had served the drinks the captain said, "Okay, out!"

"Oooo . . . " Baradja started.

But Krasser would have none of it. "Get out, both of you! Don't you know any better? Flaunting your tits in front of a man of the cloth! Scram!"

Pouting, the girls sashayed out of the messroom, leaving the clergyman pop-eyed. He glared at the captain and said, in a tightly controlled voice, "I'm afraid you and I will have to have a serious talk before I can bring my flock on board."

"Reverend," Krasser said, "I hate to disappoint you, but you're not bringing any flock on board. I have no room for passengers. Somebody else will pick you up. Don't worry, somebody will. Cheers."

The clergyman gaped at him uncomprehendingly. "I—I *beg* your pardon? You're *not* prepared to pick up my people?"

"That's right. Now finish your drink and clear out."

"But—but that's not possible!" the clergyman cried, recovering. "You can't *do* this! I—I'll have the Navy—the Army—I'll—the police!"

"Sorry," Krasser said, and knocked back his drink.

The clergyman swallowed. "But I have women, innocent children, old people more dead than alive! If you don't take them on they are doomed!"

56

"Sorry." Krasser poured himself a new one.

"But what do you want me to *do?* What do you—This is inhuman!"

"Try some more praying," Krasser said. "Now, if you'll excuse me?" He lay down, disappearing behind the table.

"But—but this is not *possible!*" the clergyman cried, panic in his voice. "You can't *do* this! What is it you want? Money? You'll have money! We'll give you all the money we have!"

"Okay, Reverend, get out."

"Some of the women have diamonds! There are watches! I'm sure that once we arrive somewhere safe, those who have money in banks will give it to you! All of it! You'll be rich!"

Without rising, Krasser called, "Kwan Chan!" The Chinese mate instantly appeared in the doorway. "See the gentleman to the rope ladder and make sure he leaves the ship."

"Very well, *tuan.*"

There was a silence; then the minister said, preposterously, "I don't know what turned you into what you are, brother, but I hope God will show mercy on your soul!" He stalked out, ignoring the Chinese.

Krasser, realizing that his nap was done for, sat upright once more and poured himself a third glass of rotgut. As the fire seared his gullet, it dawned on him that to hide out in the Pond of the Dead was not going to work. He had overlooked the obvious effect of the bombing of towns inland: the jungle must be swarming with refugees right now. Most of them would not make it, but some stragglers like these would manage to reach the coast. The Japanese were sure to start mopping them up the moment they had their hands free. Patrols would be scouring the beaches; the *Henny,* camouflaged or not, would be a sitting duck on that pond. By the fourth glass, he had decided that to hide out there for months was going to be a boring business anyhow. What would there be for him to do? Fool around with the girls, teach his mynah bird a few more blasphemies and his dog more tricks? It seemed a good working description of hell. But where else could he go?

He waddled to his cabin, pulled on a pair of khaki pants, flip-flopped to the chartroom in his slippers, climbed onto the stool, then onto the chart table and pulled out the general chart of the Archipelago. The logical goal would be Java, which the Dutch and their allies would defend to the last. But the Dutch authorities were likely to be out for his skin now, after his escape from Tarakan. The fact that he had not killed the corporal and his soldiers but just knocked them cold and set them adrift in a raft might not be considered a mitigating circumstance. Come to think of it, if he was indeed planning to head for Java, he would do well to build up some goodwill by taking on refugees. The authorities might be sore at him, but it would be difficult to string up a humanitarian who had camouflaged his ship in order to pick up refugees on the beaches of Borneo and transport them to safety.

But if he were to reach Java, his ship would be requisitioned for wartime duty. It would mean the end of the neutrality of his little Switzerland. Australia too was involved in the war; South America was the nearest neutral landfall, but to cross the Pacific was impossible without refueling in ports at war—unless he took on all the coal from the dump in the Pond of the Dead. There was enough there to see him across the Pacific. But even if he were the world's best sailor, the old bucket would never make it. One good gale and down she would go. She was a coaster, and an antique one to boot. It would have to be Java after all.

He went to the messroom, poured himself another glass, waddled onto the lower bridge and climbed onto the box of lifebelts to see what was going on ashore. Even without binoculars he could see that the people huddled together among the jetsam on the beach were in poor shape. Some of them were stretched out with exhaustion, others clustered in a small group that seemed to consist mainly of children. On the shore lay a yellow rubber raft which they must have lugged with them through the jungle. The clergyman stood haranguing his congregation, making gestures at the sky, alternating with sweeps at the ship. Krasser could tell what he was doing; he himself had given a sermon once, just for a lark, standing on a table in Madame Brandel's brothel in Banjermasin one Easter morning. He had treated the assembled girls to such a convincing parody of a sermon that when he happened to look around he saw behind his back a small crowd of customers, looking pious.

Some of Pastor Zandstra's flock had gone down on their knees when a smallish man detached himself from the crowd, got into the raft and started to paddle toward the ship. Captain Krasser watched him through the binoculars; there was something familiar about him. As the boat drew closer he recognized an old acquaintance: Jaap Stotyn, a middle-aged planter who had a small spread on the outskirts of Tjelok Barung. He had been the one to tip him off, years ago, that Madame Brandel was about to retire and sell her establishment lock, stock and barrel. Thanks to Stotyn, he had been able to buy the mynah bird before it was auctioned off. He had also picked up the two girls.

Stotyn, paddling clumsily in his raft, got close to the ship and gazed up at the faces peering down at him. He looked haggard and unshaven, a sorry sight for one who used to be so spruce and trim. While the clergyman held forth at him in the messroom, Krasser had remained unmoved; Stotyn paddling toward him with that hangdog face got to him. He looked like a sad old Fifi.

Kwan Chan lowered the rope ladder and helped Stotyn climb over the rail. The poor guy could barely stand; his clothes were torn, a festering wound on his left knee showed through a tear in his khaki trousers, his right boot was held together with string. The moment he set eyes on Krasser, however, he straightened his back, squared his shoulders, gave a jaunty wink and said, "Hello there! Long time no see!"

"Come in," Krasser said. "You look like you need a drink."

"Splendid idea! Lead the way."

At the messroom table, the captain poured two glasses, raised his and said, "Here's mud in your eye."

"Cheers, old cock!" Stotyn knocked back his. It must have been a while since his last one, for his eyes bulged and beads of sweat appeared on his forehead. "Woof!" he said. "What the hell *is* this?"

"Mixture of my own," the captain said. "Another one?"

"Not right now, thanks," Stotyn replied. Then he continued in a casual tone, "Say, what have you done to poor old Zandstra? He came back with some fantastic story about you refusing to take us on."

"He's nuts," Krasser lied without batting an eyelid. "I said I wouldn't take *him* on." His decision was made: they would be a pain in the ass to have on board and he cursed his bad luck for having stumbled upon them, but all things considered, he couldn't turn his back on them and leave them to be picked up by the Japanese. That sky-pilot was another matter; he was prepared to sacrifice his privacy, not his principles.

Stotyn gazed intently at the dwarf. "What do you mean, you won't take him on?"

Krasser poured two more glasses. "It has been my practice for many years to take pilgrims but not their leaders. I don't care what they are: nuns, pastors, priests, they all spell trouble and I won't touch 'em. I'll take your bunch, but without the clergyman. Let him stay behind and pray for wings." He knocked back his drink.

Stotyn looked at him, stunned. Like everyone else in Borneo, he was familiar with mad Krasser's aggressive atheism, but he'd never taken it seriously. "I think you are making a mistake in his case, Krasser," he said cautiously, as if to a lunatic.

"Zandstra is not your run-of-the-mill parson. He's an extraordinary man. Without him, we wouldn't have made it to the coast. He literally carried us all through the wilderness with—with his inner strength. His faith."

Stotyn's adulation of the man only hardened Krasser in his decision. To take on that clergyman would mean to take on a rival for his power. Deck passengers were okay only as long as they were cowed, obedient, accepting him as sole authority on board. "No, Stotyn," he said. "This joker started to lay down the law the moment he came in here. Separate the men from the women, clear a space on deck for church services, give him a corner for religious education of the kiddies, fish on Friday, no booze—but when my two girls came in showing their goods you could have used his nostrils for a vacuum cleaner. If I allow him on board he'll try to take over command before the day is done. And let me tell you: you need *me* now, not him. This trip is going to be no picnic; our chances of getting to Java in one piece are one in a hundred. If you want to get there, you'll have to get there on my terms. On board this ship I am God."

Stotyn smiled. "Come, come, Krasser! I'm sure Pastor Zandstra won't interfere with the running of the ship!"

"No deal. The only way you could keep that megalomaniac from interfering is by putting his head in a bucket. So, you and the rest of your party may come on board, but he stays where he is."

Stotyn started to sing the clergyman's praises again: the Reverend Zandstra this, the Reverend Zandstra that. Finally he got carried away. "I confess, Krasser, I've never been one for religion, but these last few days have made me wonder. I know how you feel about it, but, I tell you, the faith of that man is infectious. I don't think there's a single agnostic left in our group, after witnessing the power of Zandstra's faith. Despite all we went through, he never gave up and went on saying that God would save us. He was right."

It was sickening. Krasser liked Stotyn, but this made him want to throw up. He poured himself another drink, saying, "Wake up, friend! The man's a fraud just like the rest of them. Take away his God, and what . . . " Suddenly he froze, cork in hand, staring into space, as the idea struck him. Here was his chance, at last! Generations of planters and *totoks*—tender-feet—had sniggered at his principles and called him a buffoon; here was his chance to show them, to *prove* that all sky-pilots were liars and hypocrites, that all religion was superstition, nurtured by them for their own selfish ends, and that when it came to the crunch they would deny their God rather than risk their necks.

Stotyn looked at him curiously and asked, "What is it? Are you all right?"

"I certainly am," Krasser said. He slammed the cork back into the bottle. "Sure you don't want another one?"

"Look, Krasser," Stotyn said. "Don't you see—"

"Don't waste your breath. You've convinced me. I'll take him on. Go ashore and tell your people we'll be over to pick them up."

Stotyn gave him a searching look, rose and went to the door. At the door he said, "Thanks, Krasser. I knew you'd come around." But he sounded as if he suspected there might be a catch somewhere.

Krasser raised his glass. After Stotyn had left he knocked it back, wiped his mouth, slid off the seat and went to his cabin. There he broke out his number-one uniform, shaved, washed, powdered his underarms with the girls' talcum powder called *Heaven Scent* and put on his shore cap.

Amu was sitting in the bunk, painting her toenails. "Where are you going, Benji?" she asked in her singsong Malay.

"None of your business."

Baradja was plucking her eyebrows in front of the mirror over the washstand. "When are we leaving?"

He did not answer.

"Why are you all dressed up?" Baradja insisted.

He put on his cap and called out the door, "Kwan Chan! Lower number-one boat! Put six men in there with guns!"

"Guns?" Amu asked, looking up from her toenails. "Are you going hunting?"

"Get dressed," he grunted, "we've got company coming." He stepped across the high threshold onto the bridge and closed the door behind him.

On a shelf over the table in the chartroom were his Pilots, his almanac and his atheist library, which ran the gamut from *Jesus, God or Fraud?* to *Heavenly Whores: Memoirs from a Nunnery.* He swung himself onto the table, took out his Bible dog-eared with use, its margins filled with annotations like *Haha!* and *The size of a whale's gullet is three inches!* He put it in the side pocket of his tunic, looked at himself appraisingly in the reflecting glass of the Certificate of Seaworthiness, then went to the sloop deck, where the starboard boat was being swung out. Kwan Chan wanted to join the six sailors with guns and take over command, but Krasser ordered him to stay where he was. That was all he needed: to be left behind on that beach instead of the sky-pilot.

9

The prow of the boat ground ashore on the pebbles of the beach, and the dwarf from the freighter jumped out and waddled toward the Reverend Zandstra, ignoring the cheers, the hands that touched him, the tear-choked voices thanking him, a woman even bending down to kiss his cheek.

Pastor Zandstra watched the misshapen creature's approach with a smile of Christian forgiveness, but a hint of apprehension.

"I want a word with you," the dwarf said dourly. His breath smelled of gin.

"Oh? Sure."

"Over there." Krasser pointed at the far end of the beach. "It's private."

Pastor Zandstra was loath to leave his people, who were beginning to clamber on board the boat. He was, after all, personally responsible for every one of them, having nursed them through the nightmarish hardship of the past ten days. But he decided to humor the dwarf who, in God's mysterious way, had been granted the power to save them.

When they reached the edge of the jungle, out of earshot of the others, he asked, "Well? What can I do for you?"

The captain pulled a dog-eared book from his pocket. "I'm taking the others on board. I'm prepared to take you too, on one condition."

"Ah?"

"You shall, in front of your entire congregation, put your left hand on this Bible, raise your right hand and repeat after me: 'God does not exist. All religion is superstition. I am a liar and a hypocrite.' After that, you're welcome on board. But the moment you start to throw your weight around I'll have you put back ashore."

Pastor Zandstra stared at him, flabbergasted. "I *beg* your pardon?"

"Take it or leave it, just as you please." The dwarf turned and waddled toward the boat.

Zandstra's first reaction was outrage. "I—I'll do nothing of the sort!" he cried. "I—I wouldn't dream of it!"

The captain stopped and looked back at him. "That's okay with me," he said. "Goodbye, Reverend. Have fun."

Zandstra, suddenly overcome by panic, waded after the man through the hot, soft sand. He overtook him halfway to the boat and grabbed his arm. "You can't be serious!" he cried. "What have I done to you to—to deserve this?"

The little man removed the hand from his arm. "You heard me. If you want to come on board, swear that oath. If you won't, start praying."

Zandstra grabbed his arm again. "You can't ask that of me!" he cried, his voice shrill with panic. "It's—it would be blasphemy! You cannot ask a man who has devoted his life to God's service to forsake—"

"Reverend," the captain said with cold passion, "your magic formulas won't get you anywhere. I see right through them. But most people are blind, and I have tried for a lifetime to open their eyes for them. For years I've looked for an opportunity to *prove* to them, beyond doubt, that you clergy are a bunch of voodoo-spouting witch doctors; now, here's my chance! After thirty years I can *prove* it! You think I'd let you wheedle me out of an opportunity I've waited for all my life? So: swear the oath, confess for all to hear what a hypocrite you are—or the hell with you, Reverend." He turned away and waddled on toward the boat.

After a moment Zandstra cried, "Stop! Stop, everybody!" He plowed past the madman, his breath laboring, his heart in his throat. "Stop, everybody! We're not leaving! Stop!"

The dwarf pulled out a whistle and blew it; sailors jumped out of the boat, guns in hand, and barred Zandstra's way. His people, already in the boat, watched wide-eyed, but did nothing.

"He wants to leave me behind!" Zandstra cried. "He is a madman! He wants—"

The captain said to his sailors, "All right, push off. *Ajo lekas!*" He nimbly climbed on board, sat down among the bemused congregation; the boat backed away from the beach, towing the yellow rubber raft full of people.

"Don't go! Stop!" Zandstra cried, frantic now. "He's mad! Don't leave me behind!"

A few of the women started to protest; Jaap Stotyn said, "Krasser, don't be a—"

"Shut up!" the captain shouted. "All of you! If you want to sail with me, you sail on *my* terms, understood? If you don't like them, you can join him on the beach!"

"We can't permit this!" a woman cried at the bewildered group packed together on the seats. "After all he has done for us, we cannot abandon him! Take me back!" She rose and shook one of the Chinese oarsmen by the shoulder. "Take me back!"

"Come, Mrs. de Winter," Jaap Stotyn said, with the reasonable voice of Judas. "First, let's get the others safely on board ship, then you and I will have it out with the captain. I'm sure he'll see reason. Please, sit down."

She obeyed, muttering. The others said nothing.

Zandstra went down on his knees on the empty beach, his face in his hands. He heard the soft splashing of oars draw away into the distance. This could not be true! It was a nightmare! He'd wake up, any moment now! Yet, somehow, he could not convince himself it was a nightmare. It *was* true. They had abandoned him.

All he could do was pray; but no words formed in his mind. Even so, his panic subsided gradually until he was stripped of all pretense, all hubris, all sense of power, and lay, alone and helpless, on his knees before God.

He was too emotionally depleted to think in abstract terms; what he went through was a mystical experience, the awareness of the presence of God. He felt enveloped by love and tenderness. Yet he knew he was faced with a choice that would determine his relationship with God for the rest of his living days, and for all eternity thereafter. *Verily, verily I say unto thee: the cock shall not crow, until thou hast denied me thrice.* Yet Peter had lived on to become the father of the church, Christ's vicar on earth. A man so obviously flawed and cowardly had been appointed caretaker of Christ's legacy.

It had always seemed to him that, had he himself been put to the test, he would not have forsaken his Saviour but bravely stood up to his Roman challengers. Now, here he was: faced by the choice to either deny his Saviour or remain behind, martyr to his faith, certain to die of starvation or at the hands of the Japanese.

Why had God done this to him? What did God want of him? What was His will?

It was as if the question drew him away from the mystical experience, away from the sense of inadequacy and unworthiness that had, somehow, brought about the vibrant presence of God. On a rational plane, no oath would be considered valid that was sworn under duress. Like a confession extracted under torture, it satisfied only some sadistic need in the torturer himself. Of course God, like any sane, rational person, would accept that this was not a case of either denying or honoring Him—the evil dwarf was quite clearly insane; it would quite clearly be a situation of *vi coactus*. And then there was the matter of his responsibility toward his congregation, the helpless flock entrusted to his care by God Himself. There could be no doubt that during these past days God had sustained him. He could never have found the strength, never, never have risen above himself without the Holy Spirit. He had been, literally, the embodiment of Christ among this small band of people lost in the wilderness. He could not desert them now.

No one would blame him if he were to do the man's bidding in order to remain the shepherd of his flock. God would forgive him. God would understand. God would not force him to desert his congregation in their hour of need. It might even be a sacrifice God demanded of him.

When, finally, he rose to his feet and waved, shouting between his hands, "I'll do it, I'll do it!" he had convinced himself that this was the only thing to do. But he was no longer the humble, unworthy mystic who, kneeling in the hot sand at the depth of his damnation, had experienced the Love that passeth all understanding.

How could the theological justification of his swearing the oath remove him from the mystical Presence? That question he would have to answer at some later date; for the moment his task was clear: even at the possible cost of his own soul, he must not abandon those entrusted to his care.

He shouted, waved, yodeled, but no answer came from the camouflaged vessel anchored in the bay.

Terror gripped him and he fell on his knees once more, aghast.

10

It had been quite a task to make those refugees, weak as they were, climb the long rope ladder to the rail, where they were hauled on board by Kwan Chan and the cook. When finally the boat was empty it was hauled in too, the deflated raft inside.

The sky-pilot on the beach knelt on the sand, his face in his hands; after a casual glance at him the captain waddled off to the messroom. The passengers, bewildered, followed Kwan Chan, who took them to the deck allotted to them. They were clearly upset by what had happened to their shepherd and whispered uneasily to each other, but there was no protest and they settled down among the wilting greenery of the camouflage.

Meanwhile, Krasser had opened up a fresh bottle of gin and was enjoying his second glass, rolling small mouthfuls of it on his tongue, when Kwan Chan knocked on the doorpost. *"Tuan . . . "*

"Yes?"

"Man signaling from beach."

"Okay. Lower number-one boat, let the bo'sun pick him up."

"Very well, *tuan.*"

Baradja stuck her head around the door to the cabin. "What's going on?" she asked. "Who are those people?"

"Passengers," Krasser said.

"Are they going to camp out on deck?" Amu asked, over Baradja's shoulder.

Krasser looked at them with exasperation. "What are you two doing standing there? Know what the time is? Set the table!"

Baradja stepped over the threshold, sidled up to him, kissed the top of his head and said, "Don't boo at me."

She was fondling him when a whistle sounded outside. Krasser finished his drink, jumped off the seat and waddled onto the deck. The boat with the clergyman was approaching. He took up position at the top of the gangway and called over his shoulder, "Kwan Chan!"

"Yes, *tuan?*"

"Round up the passengers. I want everybody here."

"Very well, *tuan.*"

Shouting, the Chinese crew started to round up the refugees. By the time Zandstra's head appeared above the rail his flock was there waiting for him—cowed, apprehensive.

Kwan Chan helped the man over the rail, and Krasser produced his Bible. When they were standing opposite each other he asked, "Ready to swear?"

The pastor swallowed and said with a strained voice, "I want to explain to my people—"

"No mumbo-jumbo!" Krasser snapped. "Put your left hand on this Bible."

The clergyman obeyed.

"Raise your right hand."

He did, closing his eyes.

"Repeat after me: God does not exist."

"God—God does not exist."

"All religion is superstition."

"All religion is superstition."

"I'm a liar and a hypocrite."

The man opened his eyes, gave Krasser a wrathful look, but whispered, "I'm a liar and a hypocrite."

Krasser pocketed his Bible. "All right," he said, "so far, so good. But mind you: no rabble-rousing. The moment you start any of that, back ashore you go. You wouldn't be the first I've made walk the plank. The rest of you: dismiss!"

The other passengers, to whom the captain was now obviously another aspect of the lunacy of war, hurried out of sight, some women hugging their children protectively.

When Krasser entered the messroom and peered onto the table, he saw it was laid for four. "Who's that for?" he asked, pointing at the extra plate.

"That nice man," Baradja said.

"Which one?"

"You know: your friend. Mr. Stotyn."

"He's not eating with us."

His behavior mystified Baradja; the younger Amu, who hovered in the background, was unsure of his mood too, as was Fifi.

"Are you done for the day?" Baradja asked warily, after a silence.

"Yes," he said. "Now go and get the grub." When he was alone he rubbed his hands.

Reassured, Fifi came in, her claws ticking on the linoleum.

PART TWO

The Crucible

1   The straggling column of men from Rauwatta reached the foothills of the mountains on the evening of the second day. Sam Hendriks, who led the column with his old Dyak guide, put the decision to the vote as to whether to stop for a rest or to push on. Although they were so exhausted by now that they were ready to drop, the men voted unanimously to push on into the mountains, in order to shake off the native refugees that clung to them like leeches.

At first, as they tramped through the outskirts of the town and the outlying kampongs, they had been greeted with open derision by the natives squatting on the porches of their hovels or standing in groups by the side of the road. But as they got farther and farther away from the city they were followed by panic-stricken women carrying yokes, pushing carts piled high with their belongings, pulling along whining children, trailed by emaciated dogs. Soon the column became a disorderly crowd that threatened to turn the evacuation into a rout. The men walked faster and faster, trying without success to shake those carts and bands of children which could so easily be spotted from the air. Now they had to push on, just to shake the leeches.

Sam Hendriks warned them that it would be a long haul, but nobody heeded his warning. Herman expected jolly Mr. Imhof, a liquor merchant who had deteriorated into a wheedling, repulsive toddler, to remain seated by the roadside and declare that he wouldn't go another step, but even he rose to his feet and plodded on, gazing ahead like a sleepwalker at the mountain ridge above them, burnished by the setting sun. The mountains looked forbidding; the top of the ridge was bare of vegetation, a jagged rampart of granite. But at least there they would be free of the ragtag army of women and children.

Sam Hendriks proved to be a born leader. He inspired self-confidence in everyone in the column of exhausted men stumbling toward their fate in the moon landscape of the mountains. The old Dyak guide turned out to be his native overseer, as bald as a ball, and disease had turned one of his eyes into a milky marble. This, combined with two yellow eyeteeth that dug into his purple lower lip, gave him the aspect of a demon released from a bottle. His feet were scaly, flat and large; he waded rather than walked at the head of the column. When the torrid heat made the world quiver and set the other men reeling, the bald old man at the head of the column seemed to exude an evil glee until everyone became secretly convinced that they were being led into an ambush. Sam Hendriks assured them several times a day that the guide was the best in Borneo, devoted to the white man, and that he knew the mountains like the back of his hand; under his expert guidance they would reach the coast in less than a week.

No one asked: 'And then what?' Suppose they did reach the coast, what good would it do them? Sam Hendriks, however, seemed so sure of himself, and of a radiant goal of peace and security at the end of their purgatory, that they surrendered to his virile optimism.

To most of them this was their first experience of the wilderness. They had arrived in Rauwatta by plane after peering down for hours on the endless rain forest; after their arrival they had forgotten about it. They had driven about in cars, sipped Dutch gin in a club cooled by ceiling fans, all they had ever seen of the jungle was the domesticated banyan trees lining the streets and the bougainvillea climbing the wall of the clubhouse. Now they suddenly found themselves robbed of all creaturely comforts, as in the summer camps of their boyhood. They remembered rites like cutting your toenails square, never puncturing a blister, rinsing your mouth with water and spitting it out because swallowing it would increase perspiration. To Herman, the most vivid memory of life in summer camp was the weary boredom of trotting behind the leader on seemingly endless nature rambles, dreaming of ice cream, chocolate and bed.

Jolly Mr. Imhof plummeted deepest into the past: he whined and waddled, all of four years old, ahead of Herman in the single file of men. He stopped whining, however, when they started to climb. The trail was steep and uneven; soon the entire column fell silent as it slowly trudged up the cruel mountainside in the fading light, accompanied only by the rustle and rumble of pieces of rock dislodged by slipping feet. Herman, who had been thinking of Mrs. Bohm as someone he vaguely remembered from a disturbing night's sleep, was overcome with gratitude toward her as he discovered the benefits of the alpenstock. *Hit's curious all a body see, a-walking by his lone, outlandish birds and beasties' prints and traces in a stone.* The farther he stumbled and scrambled away from her, the more nostalgic her image became: an idealized vision of tender concern and quiet fortitude combined with lusty celebrations of the rites of the flesh—a dreamlike combination of earth-mother and jackbooted nanny which had as much foundation in reality, no doubt, as the dream tigers of Rousseau *le douanier*.

A shrouded moon rose from the steaming jungle below, but it soon vanished in fog. Presently they seemed to stumble through a cloud. After what seemed like hours, they stopped at a hushed command passed down the column and dropped where they stood. Sam Hendriks went wearily along the line of exhausted men and tried to cheer them up by saying they had broken the back of it now. A few more hours and they would reach the Rokul road, which they must cross before dawn. On the other side of it they would camp for the day in a lovely hidden valley with a river and lots of bananas; he had been there many times, on weekend outings with guests. He elaborated on those outings enthusiastically in an effort to make the lunar landscape appear domesticated. But his worn-out followers were beyond caring, reduced to cattle ready to rise at a shout and the poke of a sharp stick, and to amble on blindly until ordered to stop.

After a brief rest Sam Hendriks set the column in motion once more and they resumed their nightmarish stumbling through the cloud. They all clung to the one image that mattered: the back of the man ahead. In Herman's case it was that of Mr. Imhof, who had taken off his shirt. He came to know the little man's bare back intimately; more intimately, he felt, than Mrs. Imhof did: a babyish back with pink skin, a couple of defenseless moles and a row of dimples down the spine. For hours he stared at it as it bobbed and swayed before his eyes in the pale, shadowless light of the moonlit cloud. To presume that God had created Mr. Imhof in His own image appeared a sacrilege. The very concept of God seemed distant and impersonal that night; in flashes of superconsciousness Herman occasionally observed himself: struggling ant in a file of ants scrabbling across blades of grass, pieces of gravel, puddles of muddy water, driven by some life-force turned suicidal. But then he woke up to reality: Mr. Imhof stumbling ahead of him, a cuddly cherub whom he imagined being fed maraschino cherries in bed by a plump little wife. Human love when viewed on the small, pale screen of Mr. Imhof's moonlit back became copulation of two toadlike creatures darkly driven to perpetuate a pointless species. He could not visualize Mr. Imhof and his wife embracing with the passion and the fury of tigers, or even the motionless suction of mollusks. They were sexless, overweight cherubs like those that Rubens used to turn out by the score, holding up brocade curtains, opening clouds for Aurora as she came down a flight of marble steps to welcome the French Ambassador. He mused about Rubens' panoplies of overweight females thrown stark naked into gatherings of stolid burghers. He saw in his mind's eye the stocky painter scramble up a scaffolding to add some more flying babies to his version of the Annunciation: a Flemish baker informing a woman customer of a special offer of Easter breadrolls. He remembered old Professor Hennings' raptures over that painting during a lecture in his series *Theology in Art.* The frail old man with his white goatee and traces of a bachelor's breakfast on his tie came back vividly: his pale hands stretched out toward the ceiling of the lecture room as he whispered, in the throes of some private revelation, "There it is, gentlemen, the basic concept of Christianity, new on this planet: man rising from primeval darkness, God descending from above to meet him, mortality fused with immortality." Inspiring at the time; but seen from the midnight slope of a mountain in Borneo, the revelation became the raving of a lunatic. Where did "God" fuse with Rubens' winged piglet? Where was the miraculous revelation in the Flemish peasant girl's plump countenance as she stared with blank eyes at the angel from United Bakeries? Maybe Rubens had not painted it himself; he had exploited a crew of underpaid apprentices to apply flesh to his lascivious sweeps of charcoal on the gray canvas. Only one little corner of the canvas had been filled so far: a pink, plump little back, running away from death without ever seeming to advance an inch on its pointless flight. To shake the hallucination, Herman looked away from Mr. Imhof's back and turned to see how the man behind him, Mr. Palstra the pharmacist, was doing. His heart skipped a beat when he realized that there was no one behind him.

He should call out at once, warn those ahead! But he did not. His reasons were confused, akin to panic; it seemed, obscurely, his fault; surely they would stop soon and the others would catch up with them. There also was a small frantic voice, which whispered, 'Go on! Don't say anything! Go on!' If he stopped the column, the Dyak guide would have to go back to find the others and that might take hours, endangering all of them. Hendriks had said they must cross the Rokul road before dawn. Maybe what drove him on was simply the mindless momentum of the herd. Anyhow, he kept the secret of the single file being broken to himself; maybe it would go away if he refused to acknowledge it.

They stopped just before daybreak. Sam Hendriks went down the column to explain that they had now reached the road; they must cross it before sunrise, as by then it might be patrolled by the Japanese. They would cross it in about fifteen minutes, as soon as the Dyak guide could see his way in the darkness of the misty valley to the other side. "Right-o, men! You have a quarter-hour's break! Make the most of it! Where's Palstra?"

Herman looked around.

"Jesus Christ! Where's Palstra?" Hendriks cried with a screech in his voice, which so far had been calm and controlled. "Where's the rest?!"

"I—er—" Herman said. "They should be here . . . "

"They aren't! Didn't you hear him call or something?"

"No . . . "

"God damn it, this buggers us up good and proper! Arula! Come here!"

The old Dyak came trotting out of the blue of the early dawn. Hendriks went to meet him; they stood whispering urgently for a few minutes. None of the others paid any attention; the men had once more dropped where they stood and lay, motionless with exhaustion, scattered about the rocks. Little Mr. Imhof lay crumpled at the foot of a coffin-shaped boulder, his knees drawn up in the fetal position, fast asleep.

"Listen, everybody! Hendriks called, suddenly. "We have lost half our party! It's up to you to decide what we do next. We can cross the road now and leave it to Arula to go back for them after, or we can wait here while Arula goes back now to round them up. What do you want to do?"

Nobody stirred. They just lay there, oblivious of conscience, comradeship, choice.

"Those who vote to go on, raise your hands!" Hendriks cried in the dawn.

Nobody moved.

"All right," he said. "It's the decent thing to do, I suppose. Arula, go find them."

Herman realized dispassionately that this was madness. The Dyak should guide them across the road first, then go back to find the others. Already the growing daylight revealed their position: a line of bodies in a dry creek-bed on a rocky slope at the bottom of which, still in darkness, must be the road. They would be visible to any early patrol that came down the road. He should run for shelter while he had the chance. But his body did not react to the command of his reason. Like the others, he was beyond caring, part of a herd; he was incapable of making any personal choice after this descent into anonymity. Like a cow, he dozed off where he lay.

An hour later the old Dyak came back, leading Palstra and

the rest of the exhausted stragglers. By then it was broad daylight. Hendriks tried to get the column to its feet, crying, "Come on, men! Get up! Let's see how far we can get! Don't lose heart now! We're really there!" But he too was exhausted and his voice lacked the conviction it had carried before; nobody moved. Palstra and his men dropped and passed out like the rest of them. After a few minutes Hendriks gave up. "Okay," he said wearily, "let's make camp here. It's too late to attempt the crossing anyhow. Men! Lie still and you won't be seen!"

They lay still among the rocks of the creek-bed. The sun, despite the early hour, beat down on them fiercely. There would be no shade until late that afternoon, when the sun set behind the mountain ridge above them. Below them, the last clouds of morning mist began to dissipate and reveal the gray ribbon of a macadam road.

Herman lay on his back, eyes closed, mouth open. He was slowly overcome by a notion of putrefaction, as if his body were decomposing in the sun. With an effort of will he opened his burning eyes, looked up at the malevolent sky blazing with light and lifted his head with a stab of pain. His eyes slowly roved down the creek-bed, the bodies, the road, and he became aware how totally exposed they were to anyone coming down that road. They must climb back up the slope, hide from sight behind the first ridge above him. Painfully he managed to hoist himself into a squatting position, bent over and shook Mr. Imhof by the shoulder. The little man moaned and turned away to shake off the intrusion. With a sudden desperate sense of urgency, Herman rose to his knees and began to crawl upward, past the row of stretched-out bodies above him on the slope. Palstra was as oblivious to the world as Imhof, so were the others. Only one reacted like a sleeper half awakened: the fat middle-aged parson who had invoked God's blessing before their departure. He at least seemed conscious; when Herman whispered to him that they were exposed, that they must turn back and hide out of sight of the road to save their lives, the parson's bloodshot eyes vaguely discerned a silhouette above him in the burning sky. He muttered, "Please . . . So tired . . . Sleep . . . " Herman stretched out his hand to shake him, but the limp, sleeping body might roll over at his touch and start tumbling down the slope, so he let it be.

He gazed up the rocky creek-bed, desolate, devoid of shelter. Then animal fear drove him upward. He started to crawl on all fours, dragging Mrs. Bohm's alpenstock and his haversack along with him. He crawled, breath panting, heart banging in his chest, past the row of sleeping bodies, higher, higher, until he had passed the last of them. Yet something drove him on: higher, higher, beyond that ridge above, which did not seem any closer. Finally he became too tired to see straight; fierce sunlight sparkled in the tears in his eyes until they blinded him. He realized he must have a rest, grant his exhausted body a chance to recover before he crawled on. The compulsion that drove him onward was not diminished, the same inchoate, choking panic that had set him on his way was more imperative now rather than less, but his body simply could not obey it any longer. A rest. Just a brief rest . . .

He looked about him and spotted a huge, angular boulder, like a giant building block, poised in what seemed precarious balance on the rim of the narrow canyon of the creek-bed. There, in its shadow, he could hide for a few minutes, out of sight of the road. He clawed up the steep incline, sobbing with exhaustion and panic; with a final effort of will he hoisted himself over the rim into the boulder's shade. Panting, he cast a last look at the valley below, the gray road now quivering with heat, the boundless green wilderness beyond. With a grunt, he collapsed.

He was wakened by a rumble. It sounded like a freight train rolling down a track. Then a shot rang out, sending echoes reverberating around the valley. It penetrated to him that the rumble was made by cascading rocks dislodged as the others below him tried to scramble to safety.

What followed was not clear, for he froze with terror, his face in his hands. There were shots, shouts, screams, a parrot voice shouted, *"Stop! Stop, you louts! Stop!"* The staccato stutter of machine-gun fire. In the background he could hear dogs howling in frenzy.

He lay face down behind the boulder, paralyzed with fear, in a state of total helplessness. He heard a shout close by, the clatter of dislodged stones. His awareness contracted into the homicidal prayer that whoever it was might give up and roll down the creek-bed before the dogs came for him. A shot rang out, a cry of childish pain, something slithered down with a shower of stones.

After a while the shots became sparser. The barking of dogs subsided. There were no more cries, no more rolling stones. He lay behind his boulder, empty of all thoughts. It was silent.

He did not dare move for what might have been hours—he did not know. At last he slowly, secretively lifted his head and looked up. Black kites were floating in an empty sky. Vultures. He decided not to move until they came circling down; that would be the sign that there was no longer anybody about.

The vultures did not come down until nightfall. The setting sun gave the mountainside a golden hue as the last black kite vanished from the sky. He waited another half-hour or so; then, surreptitiously, he crawled out from behind the boulder and peered down the creek-bed. He saw in the rocky furrow a few indistinct blobs of white covered with black birds, which made them look hugely alive. Beyond them, across the road, he thought he saw a crouching shape bounding from boulder to boulder. The Dyak guide.

Suddenly the realization of his desperate state struck him. He leaped to his feet and cried, "Arula! Arula! Stop! Take me with you!" The vultures, wings flapping, tried to lift their gorged bodies into the air. They hopped obscenely from stone to stone until at last they were airborne and sailed up into the sky.

What they left, strewn about the bed of the gully, was bodies. Scores of them, frozen in weirdly stilted positions. Some were leaning against rocks, others sitting. Some were lying on their backs or sides, arms outstretched, or with their hands covering their faces.

Herman ventured slowly down the creek's bank. What he saw was so gruesome that he carried on as in a trance until he reached Mr. Imhof. The fat little man lay at the foot of the boulder where he had last seen him, but something was missing. His eyes.

The eyes of most of the corpses were gone. He slowly continued down the slope until he spotted Mr. Palstra. He too was without eyes; the vultures had pushed his bifocals onto his forehead to get at them. The bifocals, askew, mirrored the sun; it gave them a ghoulish life.

Slithering, crashing on his knees, scrambling back to his feet, he slid down the slope. His trousers were torn and became soaked with his blood, but he felt nothing. He crossed the road and ran blindly, in a frenzy of panic, into the wilderness on the other side.

2

When Herman came to, the next day around noon, he had no idea where he was or how long he had been lying there.

He was lying on the edge of a low cliff. Below him was a barren valley full of rocks; a stream ran through it which looked cool and inviting. With a feeling of relief he spotted a small white house on the river's bank. He slithered down the cliff, careful not to fall this time.

Seen from above, the house seemed well kept; it must be a *passang-grahan*—a government hotel for engineers of the oil company. He forgot about his cuts and abrasions, his thirst, his exhaustion, and made his way toward the house. It was closed; the doors and the shutters were tightly locked. In a sudden fury, he took his stick and beat on the door with all his might. The house derided him by refusing to sound hollow; only when his hands began to hurt and the stick to splinter did he realize, with a feeling of calamity, that he was beating on a boulder bleached white by the sun. The "house" had been a hallucination. There was no house anywhere in the barren valley, not a tree, not a blade of grass; the stream he had spotted from above had been a mirage too. The bed of the torrent that must run through this valley during the wet monsoon was dry, strewn with large, round pebbles.

He searched around the boulder for some shade, in vain. The sun was right overhead. He sat down, infinitely weary. Where was he? How long had he been wandering through this moonscape, hallucinating? He remembered crossing a silver-and-charcoal landscape overnight, huge ferns swaying among the stars. He remembered talking to people sitting at the foot of those ferns, about sin and Amsterdam and Isabel. He remembered striking a match and realizing he was talking to a mole. He remembered the mole's big pink hands gesturing in the moonlight. He remembered watching the sunrise from the entrance to a cave.

Had it really been the entrance to a cave? He leaned against the hot boulder, closed his eyes and was startled by the blood-red vortexes of his eyelids. He had to face it: his situation was desperate. Hallucinations, he had read somewhere, were nature's way of anesthetizing the dying. The mole, the ferns in the moonlight, the brook gurgling among mossy rocks were part of a dream-world without pain or thirst or discomfort, portal of death. If he wanted to survive he must get up, struggle on and try to find some shade. But he was being seduced from within to stay where he was, rest his legs caked with blood, his swollen ankles, his feet torn and sore in the shreds of his boots. He looked up; the sun was fierce and blinding. He settled down to sleep.

Pain woke him. He seemed to float overhead, looking down. He saw himself lying at the foot of the boulder, a broken doll. Somehow he had lost the animal instinct of self-preservation that had driven him on this far. He had lost everything, except a haversack and a splintered stick. He must get back inside that broken doll, return to the world of pleasant make-believe; he must struggle on or die. He picked up the haversack; it was heavy. He might as well leave it behind; there was nothing in it that could be of use to him any more. He dropped it and tried to hoist himself to his feet, but they were so sore that he decided to wait awhile and have a look inside the haversack after all. As he tried to open it he realized his fingers were swollen, his nails torn. He must have clawed up craggy slopes in the panic of the night, but he could not remember. He managed to open the sack and shook out its contents. A faint smell of peppermint. Some dirty lumps of sugar crushed in a fall. Pieces of broken glass. A cork. A crumpled brochure. *The Edible Wild Plants of the Malay Archipelago.*

He remembered Mrs. Bohm giving it to him. He visualized her face. Her eyes, Delft blue, set wide apart. The memory of her swamped him with such sorrow, such hunger for life, that he heard himself moan, a mooing sound that made him laugh: Master of Arts, University of Amsterdam, dying on a mountain-side in Borneo, mooing like a cow. Then he remembered her saying, "This little book may save your life."

He opened it at random: *Delicious treat for those who appreciate garlic. It is even better when roasted gently over a small fire, but on long marches the chewing of the small nodules will keep thirst at bay for a considerable time. Not to be confused with the giant nightshade, which is fatal, so the novice is advised not to take any risks.* A shadow passed over the page. Without looking up he knew what it was: a vulture. He dropped the booklet, grabbed the stick and said, "All right, Bohmikins, let's get the hell out of here. Down into the green, my girl." Painfully, he rose to his feet. Then he took a deep breath, said, "Tally-ho, old stick!" and staggered on across the moonscape, stumbling, groping his way with the stick like a blind man in the blinding sun. Toward the forest, old boy; toward the lush, cool jungle. The jungle was somewhere. Cool, green: long, shining leaves, giant ferns, a black-and-orange tiger with startled round eyes, with whom he would sit down and break bread as a sacrament to their creator, *le douanier.* What a pleasant way to pass through the mirror! Death as a museum, full of framed doors on pale gray walls. Doors to jungles, to the *Place du Tertre* in the rain, to the jolly crowd of naked girls having a picnic, *Déjeuner sur l'Herbe.* Which one would he choose? Old Bohmikins in some rococo bedroom, one of Renoir's bathers pinning up her hair? He had never cared for those creamy, globular blobs of feminine flesh touched with gold dust, but now that he was experiencing life in the raw, Modigliani's flat-chested, pebble-eyed females looked as dead as doornails. No—give me the fleshpots of Bohmland, the pearl-fishers of *des Indes,* catching clams like little cameras hidden by Japanese spies in the fleshpots of Egypt, the valley of Solomon's Song: *A bundle of myrrh is my well-beloved unto me; he shall lie all night betwixt my breasts.*

Yes—that's where he should go. That's where. Just a little while longer, old stick, just a little way farther, and there she would be: *Behold, thou art fair, my love; behold, thou art fair; thou hast doves' eyes.* Yes, that's what she had: doves' eyes. Good old Solomon, he had known it all.

Come, old stick: just a little way, just a little way farther across the moon, and there will be the lush jungle, the long, slender leaves, the tiger, tiger, the long, cool bed.

Behold, thou art fair, my beloved, yea, pleasant: also our bed is green.

After a long interlude of stars and sounds, of turning over and crying out, there was the dawn: blue and awesome, revealing a straight gray canal with steep banks.

He had a brief sense of awakening, a heart-stopping moment of recognition. My God! It was the road!

Miles he had walked, stumbling, falling, scrambling back onto his feet. He had crossed chasms and deserts, moonscapes and canyons, and here he was: sitting by the side of the road to Rokul, gazing into the valley below.

He could not face it. He quickly realized it was not reality, just another hallucination. He should refuse to look at the road, decide it wasn't there and concentrate on the valley. Clouds of steam roiled below; he heard a massive sound of birds, and the rumble of a freight train. The clouds filling the valley looked so soft and fleecy that he was tempted to spread his arms and take a swan dive. But he decided to rest. He knew the jungle was there. He knew he had reached it at last. All he had to do now was wait for it to reveal itself.

The clouds thinned out and began to reveal the tops of trees; self-satisfied, he began to lower himself into the jungle. It was colder than he had expected; he entered a clammy, dark cellar of foliage, through which he slithered, rustled, occasionally dangled like a monkey. Down he went, down, down, snared by creepers, tripped by roots, haunted by the warbling of birds, the chatter of monkeys, the continuous rumble of the freight train below.

The jungle became darker and darker, the undergrowth denser. He tried to keep calm, to keep the vision of the railroad track before him. Then vines snared him and caught him in their net, and he could no longer evade the knowledge that he had gone crazy in the wilderness. He was a dying madman who had been struggling gamely through a hall of mirrors and who had now reached the end of his tether. He gave up, dropped to his hands and knees and discovered, whimpering, that he could crawl under the vines that barred his way. Perhaps he would come across a path or a track, a deer run that would lead him to the railroad where the freight train rumbled. Crying, he crawled on for hours; then, with the suddenness of a fall, he found himself on the bank of a river.

A real river this time, gliding past like glass. He stared at it, overcome by exhaustion, gratitude, fear; then he saw, upstream, the white foam of rapids and understood at last where the sound of the freight train had come from.

The discovery was shattering; he would have collapsed if he had not spotted something yellow in the white bar of foam. It looked huge, alive, a wounded animal caught in the rapids, writhing in an effort to free itself. Then it penetrated to him what it was: a yellow rubber raft.

In a frenzy he threw himself into the water, lashed out blindly, plunging toward the rapids. He stumbled often, losing his balance, nearly drowning; finally, after a superhuman effort, he managed to grab a rope that was thrashing in the wild turbulence of the water. He pulled, tugged; suddenly his feet seemed to leave the ground. He drifted, weightless, wheeling, downriver, clinging to the yellow raft. He found the strength to hoist himself inside it and toppled head first into a shallow pool of water which sloshed from side to side on a thin, floppy membrane. Utterly spent, he sank into sleep.

He awoke feeling violently ill, and threw up over the edge of the raft. Vomiting cleared his mind; he acquired a sudden objectivity. He sat up and scrutinized the raft drifting downriver with the current. He saw Chinese lettering on the inside and a memory came back to him: multicolored flowers drifting down from the sky, with black seeds dangling underneath. *'We blew up the bridge, but they may parachute rafts.'* This must be one of them: the Japanese must have used it to cross the river at Rauwatta and abandoned it.

He suddenly felt hungry and tried to grab hold of some of the succulent-looking plants on the river's bank as the raft slid past. He managed to pull out a young palmetto and gnawed at its heart; someone had once said it was the edible part. It tasted foul; so he decided he was not hungry after all and used the fronds as a parasol, for each time the sunlight hit his skin it felt like boiling water.

As the day went by he developed a fever. It was not unpleasant; he talked excitedly to people in another raft that drifted by, overtaking his. He asked, shouting, who they were, and when they had died, for he realized he was dead now. One of them, an old man, shouted back that he had owned a bicycle shop in Rauwatta and been buried by a bomb; a woman was trying to finish knitting a sweater before she got to heaven. The idea of their being on their way to heaven seemed amusingly primitive, but it seemed logical that, indeed, at the end of this river there would be a reckoning, a final judgment. The dear people in the other raft seemed to assume that in their case it would be favorable; he knew that in his case it would be the reverse. He would be punished for not reporting that the column had broken behind him; he knew he was to blame for Mr. Palstra's eyeless bifocals. But there had been no malice involved, only panic and cowardice; if God were indeed pure love and mercy, He might understand, but would Imhof and Palstra and the others? Or would they be waiting for him, with their empty eye-sockets? Maybe he could hide among the people in the other raft, now rapidly passing his own. But why should he, if they had no eyes?

He threw up over the side again; when he slumped back into the pool of sloshing water he had a moment of lucidity. He realized he was not dead yet, but that life oozed out of him each time he vomited. He was getting weaker by the hour, slipping relentlessly into oblivion.

He slept intermittently. He was vaguely aware that at times the raft was bumping into snags, scraping past clusters of reeds and tresses of air roots trailing in the water. Occasionally rapids woke him; the raft was caught in them, it seemed for hours. Weak as he was, he had to push it through until the force of the water pried it loose and carried it on downstream.

He was awakened by silence. No more reeds scraped along the raft, no more overhanging boughs dragged across him, showering him with insects and dead leaves. The water no longer gurgled around fallen palm trees seesawing up and down in the current. He awakened with a sense of space, looked over the rim, saw the horizon, the sea and a little island.

He slowly drifted past it: a small island topheavy with palms and mangroves. When he got closer he thought he discerned faces among the foliage, and suddenly he recognized it—a *Jugendstil* lithograph of this same dark little island topheavy with black trees and weeping willows: Arnold Böcklin's *Isle of the Dead*. So it had not been an artist's imagination; here it was.

The current was carrying him swiftly out to sea. The island, the silent people staring at him from among the trees were his last chance to cling to life. He tried to call but produced no sound, to stand up and wave but his legs refused to support him, to paddle with his hands but they were powerless against the current. He cried out but his cry was as feeble as a bird's, lost in the vast emptiness of the sky and the sea.

He closed his eyes. This was the end. "Father," he said, "into Thy hands I commend my spirit." But even in this ultimate moment he knew it was merely a literary phrase. As he had lived, so he would die: a phrasemaker.

What would it be like? A fusing with the light, the sky? An evaporation of his personality? Whatever it would be, he had better prepare himself.

He stretched out in the warm slop on the bottom of the raft. The sunlight burned his face cruelly. He groped for the palm frond, put it over his face and waited, in utter surrender. Suddenly something hit the raft; he was violently shaken.

He threw aside the palm frond. The bow of a boat loomed over him. He croaked, "Help!"

Hands dragged him into the boat; he clung to a man's thin, muscular leg as he slumped on the bottom; the man was a Chinese. The boat moved into the shade, bumped against a wall. A rope ladder led up the sheer cliff; faces were peering down on him. He was pulled to his feet but could not stand up, let alone climb the ladder. A rope was lowered and looped under his arms; then he was hauled up, crying. His face was wet with tears when he arrived at a gate. A white dwarf asked, "And what have we here?"

With a last mortal slyness he answered, "Herman Winsum, religious editor of the *Borneo Times.*"

"Ah ha!" the dwarf cried. "Another theologian! I'll be right back!"

He lay waiting on hot iron, faint and sick.

The dwarf came back. "All right, put your left hand on this Bible, raise your right and repeat after me: God does not exist."

Although he knew it was part of a hallucination, he said, hoarse with tears, "God does not exist."

"Religion is superstition."

He licked his lips and tried to mouth the words, but it took more effort than he was able to put out. Finally he managed to whisper them, barely audible.

"I'm a liar and a hypocrite," the voice said.

It hit him with a terrible shock: this *was* the voice of God. This *was* the truth. "Yes," he croaked, "I was a liar and a hypocrite." Then he closed his eyes and added in a whisper, "Forgive me. I was weak."

"Put him with the rest," the voice said with distaste.

Hands grabbed him and carried him off. He cried out; but all he could cry for now was his mother. He cried her name, over and over again, and thought he heard a door squeak. He saw a light in the darkness and waited, weeping, for her hand to stroke his hair, her voice to reassure him that he was safe now she was here. Then he heard a wolf whistle and a cretinous voice, *"I love yew!"*

He covered his face with his hands and realized that he was in hell.

3   The children had just finished lowing, along with Sister Ursula, *Flow Gently, Sweet Afton* when Adinda came running across the compound.

Sister Ursula saw her through the open wall of her classroom. The image seemed to have about it an indelible quality, etching itself in her memory: the sunny compound with its islands of purple shadow, the native woman running toward her, holding her sarong, hair flying. She saw Adinda lose one of her sandals but the woman did not seem to notice; she came flopping across the compound like a big, flustered bird, then crashed out of that dreamlike vision into the classroom, crying, "They are coming! They are coming!"

Sister Ursula felt a flush of gooseflesh on her arms; otherwise she was calm and composed. Now that the moment had come she had lived so often in fearsome fantasies at dead of night, she discovered that in her dreams it had been worse. In her dreams she had panicked, run away, tried to hide; the whole thing had ended in a frenzy of blind terror. Now she calmly ordered Adinda to take the children to the secret grove and wait for her there.

Adinda's mouth fell open. "But you must come!" she cried. "You don't know what they'll do to you if they find you here! You must not stay! You must come, *njonja*, you must!"

Sister Ursula suppressed a beginning of panic and said, "Don't worry about me. Jesus will protect me. Now hurry! I don't want those soldiers to find the children before I've spoken to their commanding officer."

"But, *njonja*, they are not—"

"Shush! Do as I tell you. I want them to find me here. That way I can hold them up long enough for you to hide the children. Hurry! Off with you!"

To her alarm, Adinda, who had always been so placid, started to sob hysterically; before she realized what she was doing, Sister Ursula slapped the woman's face. It worked, but it unnerved her completely. It was the beginning of violence; she herself had released the wind-blown seed of violence into the atmosphere.

After the children had left, singing, hopping, Sister Ursula knelt in the empty classroom and prayed. The moment she invoked Christ's love and put herself at the mercy of His sacred heart, she felt all fear subside. At Mission College she had shared a room with Inoma Kyushi, a charming girl; they had become close friends and she had learned a great deal about the Japanese mind. She got up and looked around the compound. It was deserted, all the natives had fled. She suddenly felt unsafe and set out for the toilet where she had hidden before.

The moment she stepped into the sunlight the whole forest sprang to life. There was a blood-chilling scream of madness and fury; all around her, strange people leaped from the bush, men in striped pajamas carrying machetes, spears and knobkerries. As they came running toward her she realized these were not

Japanese soldiers but escaped convicts; she had seen them at work on the road occasionally, chained together like beasts. Now she saw their crazed hatred as they ran toward her. She tried to outstare them, tried to bless them with a sign of the cross; when they stopped a few feet away from her, she asked in her best Malay, "Who is your leader?" Then one of them opened his pajama trousers. She turned and ran, screaming; but it was only part of her that screamed and was caught and struggled and bit and thrashed and was terribly, terribly hurt. Her real self, the true Ursula, knew that she was one with Christ, that she was going through the agonies of the crucifixion as ultimate embodiment of her calling, her privilege on earth. She was torn apart in unbearable agony, but praying "Jesus, Jesus, Jesus," she escaped from pain and horror in the euphoria of the cross.

Sister Ursula, teacher of retarded children of the Sacred Heart Educational Mission, was raped seventeen times before they dragged her almost lifeless body to the river's edge and dumped it in the reeds for the alligators.

That was where Lieutenant Hin, sent to search for her, found her when he finally dared venture near enough, after the Mission had been set on fire and the marauders had left to continue their rampage through the wilderness.

4   Sister Ursula slowly regained consciousness and opened her eyes. Above her was the deep blue sky, a furrow between dark treetops that drifted by overhead. Her first thought as she rose to the surface was for her children. Anguish hit her with such force that she tried to rise on her elbows but found she could not move. Her body was numb from the neck down and heavy, as if she lay buried in sand; all she could move was her head.

She looked sideways and saw a native soldier at the rudder of a boat. A man's face appeared above her and a voice asked, "Sister? How are you?" It was the young lieutenant.

She tried to speak but although she moved her lips there came no sound. It was as if, together with the control over her body, her voice had been taken away from her. Her eyes filled with tears; now she could no longer see either. Then a hand gently stroked her hair, it gave her a feeling of nakedness as she realized she had lost her veil.

It began to come back to her: the convict advancing on her, grabbing her, ripping her habit. She prayed in terror: 'Christ, beloved heart of Jesus, help me.' Instantly, she felt peace. The horror receded even though tumbled images of violence and the remembrance of pain persisted. She had shared Christ's ultimate torment; all she wanted now was to dissolve in that blue sky overhead, that ocean of light and love. She felt that her spirit was leaving her paralyzed, mauled body; then something held her back. It was the image of little Saïdja stumbling through the jungle, losing his shoe. She must get up, not lie there praying selfishly for deliverance from her desecrated body but get up and run back to him, run, run . . .

By running back to the children in her thoughts, she ran back to what had happened in the Mission, a horror she could not face. Anguished, dazed with shock and pain, she fell asleep.

She awakened as she was being lifted up by many hands. She recognized the faces of Father Sebastian, Reverend Mother, Sister Anna. In their eyes she saw how she looked: crushed, befouled, her veil gone, her torn habit soaked with blood. She felt an unutterable shame. Closing her eyes, she prayed desperately. She concentrated on Christ's pierced hands, His crown of thorns which as an act of grace she had been allowed to wear. But she could not recapture the euphoria she had been granted back at the Mission.

The Sisters were tender and concerned. They put up a little shelter of palm fronds on the beach to shield her from the sun. They prayed over her, assured her that she would soon be taken to a hospital. Shame crushed her; all she could do was lie there, eyes closed, buried in the sand, voiceless, sightless with tears.

Night fell. The little shelter was taken away and she lay under the night sky. When finally everyone had settled down, she opened her eyes and gazed at the stars. There was great peace in them and a feeling of eternity. With open eyes she prayed for forgiveness. She had been chosen to embody Christ and proven to be unworthy of that grace. For here she lay, worrying about the children, beset by that desperate urge to run back to them, run, instead of leaving them to God, who was aware of each falling sparrow and counted the hairs on each person's head. But she found she could not believe that the children would be saved without her. Even if Adinda had managed to round them up after they scattered in the forest, she would only have taken them back to the darkness from which they had emerged. Little Saïdja would never find his shoe.

She must have made a sound, for a silhouette appeared among the stars and a man's voice said, "Don't worry, Sister, we are right here with you. Tomorrow, at the latest the day after, we are sure to be picked up. My commanding officer knows we're here, he will send a boat. Soon you will be looked after properly. Would you like some water?"

Another silhouette appeared among the stars, and the Reverend Mother's voice said, "Thank you, lieutenant, we'll look after Sister Ursula. You go back to your post."

When at last Sister Ursula found herself alone under the stars once more, she prayed, with all her heart and all her soul, that she might be delivered from the sin of lack of faith. She prayed fervently; in the end peace descended. Christ blessed her with stillness at the center. As long as she concentrated on Christ, whose martyrdom she had been allowed to repeat in her flesh, she could keep her mind off little Saïdja stumbling through the jungle, looking for his shoe, and leave him to God.

The lieutenant had been right: when dawn broke, Sister Anna came excitedly to tell Sister Ursula that a ship had anchored in the mouth of the river overnight.

She was carried onto a dock on a makeshift stretcher. A launch left with Father Sebastian, the Reverend Mother and some of the Sisters; the others and the soldiers stayed with her, waiting for the launch to return.

It took a long time; when it came back the Reverend Mother returned with it and knelt beside the stretcher. She looked flustered. "Sister Ursula," she said in a strained voice, "you must be brave and not let yourself be upset by what is about to happen. The ship that has come to pick us up is the coaster with the awful midget who gave us such a difficult time when he brought us here four years ago. He's a depraved, lost soul who now has gone completely mad. Sister, in order to be admitted on board ship you'll have to swear a blasphemous oath."

Sister Ursula felt ill and weak. She had been united in mystic union with Jesus, lost in the contemplation of His sacred wounds; the Reverend Mother was a bewildering intrusion.

"In order to be admitted on board ship," the Reverend Mother repeated, her voice quivering, "the atheist madman demands that we all swear on his Bible that our religion is superstition, that God does not exist and that we are liars and hypocrites. Can you imagine such sacrilege? If ever I encountered the Antichrist, it is that blasphemous monster!"

What came through to Sister Ursula was the Reverend Mother's anger. It hit her like physical pain. She closed her eyes.

"Of course we did not agree at first," the Reverend Mother's angry voice continued, "but after putting it before God, Father Sebastian and I concluded that this was a case for which the Holy Church provides an answer. It is the *reservatio mentalis*. You know what that is, don't you Sister?"

Eyes closed, Sister Ursula shook her head.

"At one time or another I have called it, in my ignorance, a pious fraud. I even called it 'lying like truth.' Now I know better: it is wisdom and grace under torture. It is God's way of blessing us, His children, in our moment of greatest need. Sister, as you swear that wicked oath, say within yourself in utter humility: 'Forgive, Christ Jesus, the weakness of my flesh. My spirit adores Thee, my heart remains Thy servant, nothing of what I say can touch the truth I know in my soul.' Then the spoken words will be meaningless before God. Do you understand, Sister Ursula? You may speak the sacrilegious oath, Father Sebastian as your spiritual father has freed you to do so. Afterward, he'll take your confession and grant you absolution. Do you understand?"

To be free of the grating voice Sister Ursula nodded, eyes closed.

"Very well," the Reverend Mother said, and she rose with a rustle of her starched habit. "You may take her now."

The stretcher was lifted on board the launch with bumps and heaves that made Sister Ursula's inert body slither uncomfortably, jarring her out of her somnolent state. The boat chugged across to the ship, the flank of which presently loomed beside her. People stood looking down over the rail; ropes with slings were lowered from what seemed a giddying height, the slings were put around the stretcher and she was hauled up slowly, swaying and bumping against the wall. Finally arms reached out, pulled the stretcher over the rail and put it down on the deck. People crowded around her; she saw the white habits of the Sisters and Father Sebastian's cassock. They were shooed away by a little man in a crumpled tropical suit with a sailor's cap who came waddling toward her and bent over her.

"She looks well enough to me," he said to someone she couldn't see. "Step back, everybody!" He squatted beside her. "Well now," he said.

She tried to smile.

He gave her a searching look. His face was sharp and cruel. "Your superior says she explained to you about this. All you've got to do is put your hand on this Bible and repeat after me—"

She looked at his face above her and, smiling, shook her head.

He looked at her without interest. "Okay. Kwan Chan!"

A young Chinese joined him. "Yes, *tuan?*"

"Put this woman ashore." He moved away.

There was a hubbub of angry voices, then someone cried, "Halt! I am an officer of Her Majesty's armed forces! I command you, in the name of Queen Wilhelmina of the Netherlands, to leave this woman alone! This is an order! Don't make me use force!"

The little man said calmly, "Kwan Chan, take his popgun away and put him in the paint locker."

There were frightening sounds of a struggle: the scraping of boots, a stifled cry; she closed her eyes. Then she heard the captain's voice again, calm as before, "What about the two soldiers that came with him?"

"They are in the galley, *tuan,* eating."

"All right," the little man's voice said. "Is there anyone here who'd like to have a shot at changing this woman's mind?"

"I will do so," she heard Father Sebastian say.

"Okay. Go ahead. You've got three minutes."

Father Sebastian knelt beside the stretcher, took her hand and whispered urgently, "Sister Ursula, don't be stubborn! This man is insane, he'll take you back to the shore and abandon you. He cannot be reasoned with; I tried it, a number of priests of other faiths who are on board this ship have tried it. You *must* obey, Sister Ursula! Just speak the oath and remember the words the Reverend Mother gave you. Will you, Sister Ursula?"

She shook her head.

"Please! I beg of you in all humility. I'll take your confession afterward, I'll grant you absolution. The oath is of no consequence, Sister, mere meaningless babble as long as you speak it while thinking the thought the Reverend Mother mentioned to you. It will save your life."

She opened her eyes and whispered painfully, "I cannot deny Jesus. He *is* my life."

Father Sebastian hesitated; then he made a sign of the cross on her forehead, straightened up and disappeared from view. She heard him say, "I don't know where this voyage will end, captain, but I'll personally see to it that you are handed over to the proper authorities. You are a monster."

"No, sir!" a laughing voice cried somewhere. "He's the only one here who takes God seriously!"

The little man appeared beside her and suddenly she felt sorry for him. "I didn't mean to hurt your feelings," she said. It sounded feeble and a little silly.

He gave her a look she could not understand. He looked as if he were about to speak, then someone loomed over him, a thin, haggard man with gray hair. "Look, Krasser," he said calmly, "you're one hell of a sailor and I know that with this crowd you have to safeguard your authority, but here's a very sick woman, paralyzed from the neck down. You can't expect a paralyzed, sick woman to swear that oath of yours."

The little man contemplated her for a moment with an odd expression on his face; then he called, "Kwan Chan!"

The Chinese appeared beside him. "Yes, *tuan?*"

"Put her out for'ard by the anchor winch. Tell the lookout that nobody is to visit her or speak to her." He turned and said, "You hear that, everybody? No one shall contact this woman until after she's sworn the oath. Until then, she's in quarantine. Dismiss!"

Chinese sailors picked up the stretcher and carried her away. Behind her someone cried, "Antichrist!" It sounded like the Reverend Mother.

Sister Ursula had no idea where they were taking her and was too sick to care. She longed for it to stop: the banging into corners, the sickening heaves. Finally, somewhere at the far end of the ship where the railings came together, she was put down beside a big machine with a chain in it. A Chinese in dirty shorts and a singlet squatted on top of the machine, cleaning his toenails with a knife.

She smiled at him; the Chinese lifted the knife in greeting, then continued to clean his nails. She sank, exhausted, into giddy prayer.

5   Krasser, perched on the messroom seat, was about to toss back his second glass before supper when there was a knock on the doorpost. It was Stotyn. "May I come in?"

Krasser grunted.

"Thanks." Stotyn stepped over the high threshold, sat down and poured himself a glass. He put the cork back with a squeak and asked, "You aren't serious about that nun, are you? Leaving her out there unattended?"

Krasser gave him a stony look and uncorked the bottle again. "Was that you who cracked the joke about my taking God seriously?" he asked, pouring his third.

"No, that was Dr. Homans, the history teacher. I wish, by the way, we had a physician on board. That woman urgently needs medical care."

"She'll get all the medical care she needs from me."

"Come now, Krasser! What experience do you have nursing raped nuns?"

"I'll look it up in the paper doctor, same I do for everyone else. Now finish your drink and get out."

Stotyn rose. "You can't leave her out there unattended, Krasser," he said. "I respect your convictions, but what do they have to do with torturing the innocent?" He left.

Krasser indulged in a fourth, then slipped off the seat, waddled to the chartroom, climbed onto the table and picked from among the books on the shelf *The Ship Captain's Medical Guide*. He looked up *Rape* in the index, but there was nothing between *Ramsden eyepiece* and *Rapture of the deep*. It was not an emergency likely to occur on board ship apart from forcible buggery among Chinese crew members, who looked after themselves. Baradja and Amu clattered with crockery in the messroom; after a while Baradja stuck her head around the door and said, "Lunch in five minutes."

"Come here," Krasser said.

"But the food . . . "

"I want to ask you a question."

Baradja stepped over the threshold; Amu appeared behind her in the doorway.

"Have you ever been raped?" Krasser asked.

Baradja looked taken aback.

"I know plenty of people who have," Amu chirruped in the doorway.

"You stay out of this!"

Amu vanished in a snit.

"Would you know what to do for someone who's been raped and is now paralyzed?" Krasser continued.

"Why?"

"We have a paralyzed, raped nun on board and she needs—well—attention. You and Amu will have to look after her—change her clothing, put her on the pot, whatever."

"I don't know anything about nuns."

"A nun is a woman like any other. Go ahead, she's out on the forepeak."

"But lunch—"

"Okay, lunch. After that, get with it."

Baradja left. Krasser tapped the barometer, checked the overhead compass, then saw Fifi peer over the threshold, ears cocked, wise old peepers sizing him up, trying to divine his mood. "Okay, slut," he said. "Come in."

Reassured that the mood was mellow, she came. He picked her up and rubbed his nose against her wet, cold snout. Then he put her down and said, "Lunch! Who knows, there may be something in it for you."

Fifi hurried ahead of him to the messroom.

6

When Stotyn returned to his fellow passengers on deck, his latest bulletin was cut short by Mrs. de Winter. She came running from the galley, where she had gone to collect some food for the poor nun, crying, "My God! Do you know what I just discovered? That delicious Nanking pie!"

"What about it?" Dr. Homans inquired.

"Do you know what it's made of?"

"Don't tell me," Dr. Homans said.

"I *will* tell you!" Mrs. de Winter's eyes widened dramatically. She waited until she had everyone's attention, then she cried, aghast, "Dogfood!"

Herman Winsum turned away when the others began to express horror and indignation. He had felt an outsider from the moment he joined the refugees; now he felt disgusted. How was it possible that people who had just witnessed an example of human greatness that put them all to shame forgot about it the moment they were told their favorite Chinese dish was dogfood?

"Winsum? Seasick?" It was Zandstra, the minister from Tjelok Barung. "Not surprised; I don't feel too well either. Imagine: dogfood!"

"We all enjoyed it at the time," Herman said. "It made nobody sick."

"It certainly will now!" Zandstra cried with fervor. "I'd sooner starve than swallow one more forkful of that stuff! Who knows what's in it!"

Herman decided to speak up. "I think it's more important the nun refused to swear the oath. She put us all to shame."

Zandstra stiffened. "She was told by her superiors to swear the oath and have done with it. To their way of thinking, she endangers her soul more by refusing to submit to church discipline than by humoring a lunatic for the sake of everyone's survival."

Herman knew that he should leave well enough alone, but continued, "She showed us up for what we are: cowards of feeble faith." The "us" was a matter of courtesy.

There was a silence during which Zandstra digested that. Then he said, "I think you are laboring under a misconception, my friend. As a pastor, my first duty is to safeguard the well-being of my flock. Not to swear the oath would, in my case, have meant abandoning them. She has no flock, so she can afford martyrdom." He marched off, leaving Herman to contemplate the dazzling expanse of the sea seen through the foliage of the camouflage.

As he stood there, gazing at the empty sea, the enormity of their folly compared to the nun's lonely witness became grotesque. Here they all were, chance survivors of an apocalypse that had destroyed their world, and what did they do? Gaggle about having been tricked into eating dogfood, rather than dare to contemplate the fate that awaited them just around the corner. What was in store for this ship of fools with its carnival camouflage? Tomorrow or the day after they would run out of coastline and be forced into the open on their way to Java—or wherever they might be going. Then what? So far, they had been saved by blind chance. Why should they go on being saved? Why?

There was no intelligent answer to that question, but for some reason the nun on the foredeck seemed like a beacon of hope. He knew that it was sheer superstition, that he was falling under the spell of some tribal voodoo going back to the beginning of man's time, but it seemed of crucial importance that he speak to her. Maybe not even that—just go to her and experience again whatever mysterious power was registered by his intuition, or by the collective unconscious, or, God knew, by his soul.

Nobody was watching him; they were all huddled together in little groups, mesmerized by the pie emergency. He sidled through the palms, along the rail, toward the steps to the forecastle. He was about to go up the stairs when a stern voice called, "Winsum! Where do you think you're going?!"

It was Zandstra, glowering at him like a prison trusty. "You heard what the captain said! You'll make trouble for all of us!"

"I just thought I'd . . . "

"Come down and do as you're told! The captain said: no contact with the woman! If you want to visit her, go ask his permission first!"

"That's a thought," Herman said, wavering. "Maybe I should."

If he wanted to go to see the captain, he had better think of a valid excuse. By the time he reached the steps to the bridge he had decided he would suggest that he try convincing the nun to swear the oath. He might be a suitable person to do so as he had sworn the oath himself with delirious enthusiasm.

As he started up the steps to the bridge, fate intervened in the shape of the captain's two Dyak women, who came down the steps, one of them carrying a basin, the other towels and

110

soap. They betrayed no interest in his presence; as they passed he caught a whiff of the East: sweat, hair oil and a sweet, cloying scent which his maid had told him, eyes wide with drama, was opium. He watched them cross the deck, heading for the forecastle.

Their passing struck those on deck like a bomb. "My God!" Zandstra said, looking up from a consultation with Mr. Faber the mortician, who lay supine on the hatch. "He's sending his whores!"

Dr. Homans leered at the two bare-breasted women as they sashayed up the steps to the forepeak. "He caught you napping, Zandstra!" he cried. "One up for the atheists!"

It seemed an inopportune moment for an audience with the captain. Maybe, Herman thought, he should instead go and visit old Hin, who had been incarcerated on bread and water in the paint locker since yesterday. To visit a prisoner seemed to hold less promise for the future of his soul than to visit the nun's Golgotha, but it was better than Nanking pie.

As he made his way to the aft deck, children were playing tag among the palm trees, squealing and shouting. Mr. Faber the mortician, stretched out again on the hatch of number-one hold, rose and shouted, "Quiet, the lot of you! Stay with your mothers on the other deck, where you belong!"

Mrs. de Winter said admonishingly, "Children belong as much with their fathers as with their mothers, Mr. Faber."

"They aren't mine!" Mr. Faber snarled.

"In these apocalyptic times Everyman's children are every man's," Mrs. de Winter said unctuously.

The children squealed as they stormed past; Mr. Faber muttered and spread a handkerchief over his face; then one of the children tripped, fell and screamed blue murder. Herman hurried on his way.

7 Sister Ursula heard, on the fringe of her consciousness, the sound of children playing, a thud of someone falling, a silence and then hysterical tears. Her instinctive reaction was to get up and find out what was the matter; but she could not move her limbs. At that moment the anguish over her own children, lost in the jungle, returned with such force that she started to weep.

One of the native women who was lifting her off her litter asked, "Are we hurting you, *njonja?*"

She shook her head.

"Then why are you crying, *njonja?*" the woman asked. "Is there something I can do for you?"

She opened her eyes, blurred with tears, saw the silhouette of the woman above her and suddenly the terrible worry about her children blotted out all else. She had lain there ready to dissolve in that infinite ocean of light and love; now she was back in the jungle, calling for them, running, running . . .

"Don't worry, *njonja,*" the native nurse said. "We'll look after you." The women put her litter down on the deck with great gentleness, but she was hardly aware of it. All of her, her very self, seemed to dissolve in tears. Then a hand stroked her brow.

She didn't know what it was: its tenderness, the concern it expressed, or whether it was just a hand held out to her as she lay there awash in sorrow and despair, but it brought relief. It broke through her loneliness and sense of isolation.

The hand went on stroking her forehead, slowly, gently. She felt as if she were being led out of a valley of darkness. It was not just the comfort the kind woman radiated, it was the realization that the grace of embodying the Spirit of Christ was not confined to Catholic Sisters. And if God in His infinite mercy could send a hand to comfort her at the depth of desperation, so He would protect her little lambs astray in the wilderness.

While the two women washed her, pampered her, gave her a wonderful feeling of care and companionship, she started to talk about her children.

8

The paint locker was a rusty steel cubicle on the aft deck where the women bivouacked. The area was out of bounds to the men but a religious editor of the *Borneo Times* was as good as a minister, and the clergy had the run of the place. Nevertheless, it gave Herman a feeling of discomfort; women lay around in various stages of undress, covering themselves hastily at his approach. Mrs. de Winter lit out after him like one of Wagner's Valkyries; when she saw who he was she reluctantly granted him passage. Eyes straight ahead, with ministerial tread, he made his way to the bo'sun's locker and spoke through the small open porthole in its door into the darkness beyond. "Hin? Are you there?"

It was an idiotic question, as Hin could not possibly be anywhere else; the door was secured with chain and padlock.

Hin, incarcerated in the unventilated cubicle in what must be the temperature of a pressure cooker, cried enthusiastically, "Oh yes, thank you! Jolly decent of you to come and have a dekko!"

His ghostly face appeared in the porthole, operatically emaciated with the beginning of a beard. "What's new on the Rialto?"

"Not much. Sister Ursula is still out on the forecastle."

"The sod!" Hin, despite his prep-school language, sounded fierce. "Wait till we get to Java! I'll have that little brute in irons before you can say knife!"

Poor Hin, in his sweltering cell reeking of tar and paint, should be permitted his dreams of grandeur. "I know it's tough," Herman said vaguely, "but there's not much one can do under the circumstances, is there? To bend may be wiser than to break."

Hin growled, "I'd sooner kill him with my bare hands than kiss his ass, the swine!"

"Quite," Herman said. "Even so, I'd like to get you out of there, back into the fresh air. Let's think of—"

"The only thing I can think of," Hin snapped, "is my sister."

"Ah?" It seemed the appropriate sound to make.

"I don't want this story to get around, but she was—er—sexually assaulted by a bunch of whites at the age of nineteen. She was going to be a cellist. She was about to enter the Academy of Music in Batavia. Instead, she entered a convent."

"I'm so sorry . . . "

There was an embarrassing silence during which Hin breathed heavily through the porthole. Then he said, "Maybe now you understand why I would've killed that midget had I been able to lay hands on him."

"Who—er—did it? To your sister, I mean."

"Planters. Drunk after a party. They got off scot-free, of course. Because of lack of evidence, so-called."

"I'm so sorry."

"So, just leave me be, old boy. I'm quite happy in here, nursing my rage. How is the poor nun?"

"I don't really know. The captain's—er—companions are looking after her right now."

"Wait till we get to Java," Hin said darkly. "I'll have him strung up by his little legs in a banyan tree."

The dream of grandeur was becoming somewhat overheated; Herman looked for an excuse to withdraw. He said brightly, "I'll go and see if I can rassle up a bottle of beer for you. How'd that be?"

"Very civil of you, old boy, but don't bother. I have my daily ration of water; I'd rather go easy on the liquids. You know the adage: the more you drink, the thirstier you get."

"Well—I've got to trot along. I'll be back to see you soon."

"Please do."

"Be well, now."

"Ta-ta. Awfully civil of you, coming by."

"My pleasure." Back went the religious editor, eyes downcast, face set in compassion, sidling through the harem full of reclining females and toddlers romping like puppies on number-two hatch. As he passed her, Mrs. de Winter said, "A little later in the day would be better for visiting, Mr. Winsum. This is the hour when most young mothers are nursing. Others like to undress for their siesta."

What a pernicious busybody she was! "Thank you, Mrs. de Winter," he muttered, "I'll keep it in mind."

He went back to his lookout spot on the men's deck, by the shrouds of the foremast, to gaze at the sea through the trees and the mangroves. They were nosing inland, the smell of the jungle was all around him. Suddenly, there they were: the men of Rauwatta, staring at him through hollow sockets.

Nausea rose in his throat. He covered his face with his hands. For the first time, he realized that his life would never be the same again, that they would be with him forever, until the day he died—even, God help him, beyond.

116

9   All night Sister Ursula was aware of whispering and small sounds at the bottom of the steps that led down from the platform on which she lay. She hoped that no one would come up to hold forth at her again about swearing the blasphemous oath.

Then, just before dawn, the knowledge came to her that she was dying. It came without drama, without emotion. Death did not frighten her; it never had, not since she had taken the veil. All her loved ones would be waiting for her, even though by now she had almost forgotten their faces, so long had it been since she had last seen them. She would join the blessed and the sanctified in eternal bliss, and she was sure that the Lord would find something for a woman of her experience and practical bent to do in heaven. The one thing that darkened that happy prospect was the thought of her children.

She had accepted the inevitability of leaving them to God; there simply was nothing else she could do. She had managed, with an effort of will, to suppress the anxiety and the heartbreak that lay just below the surface of her consciousness. Now that she was about to die, maybe before the day was over, she must pray to God that He might grant her a small sign that He was indeed looking after them. But that was sinful. She should have faith, not ask for signs. She must pray instead that God would forgive her this last doubt, as it was brought about by love. All she could do was plead for her children in person when she saw Him, very soon now. She did not wonder what it would be like to meet God and His Blessed Son face to face. She had known them all her life; she did not need the miracle of encounter to heighten their reality.

She knew why she was soon to die, why her body had given up the struggle and now prepared itself for the end. It was not the pain, or the paralysis. The only thing that had kept her alive so far had been the worry about her children, the urge to *do* something. She now had accepted, at last, that there was nothing left for her to do on earth to help the little ones, nothing at all. The best she could do for them was to go to heaven as quickly as possible and plead for them at the feet of her Saviour. She would do anything, make any sacrifice that might be demanded of her, but she could only do so in heaven. Her task on earth had ended; to stay on would merely postpone her fervent personal plea to Christ.

As she lay there watching a new day being born, her last day on earth, she felt lucid and tranquil, just a little dizzy, as if she were still half immersed in a dream. When the two native amahs came to change her bed and wash her as they had done the day before, she finally woke fully in the young sunlight. She hoped that they would put her out in the sun, for she was cold.

"May we change your sheets, *njonja?*" the elder of the two women asked. The young one smiled down at her with a flash of white teeth.

She nodded and whispered, "Thank you."

118

Maybe it was their human presence, maybe the care they gave her poor mauled body, but as they started their gentle ministrations she was suddenly overcome by the urge to talk about the children again. As they worked she whispered to the two of them all about Saïdja and his shoe: how she had labored with him; his final triumph the day the planes came over; how he too must have fled into the jungle, losing his shoe.

She had to talk about it, but doing so cost her that peace and tranquillity and shattered her acceptance of the will of God. Once again she was choked with sorrow and despair; now she was back in the jungle, calling for the children, running, running.

"Don't worry, *njonja*," the younger amah said, massaging her shoulders. "Somebody will go after them."

"No, no! To Adinda they are just . . . animals . . . "

"Can't you ask somebody else to go and find them?" the girl asked, concentrating on the work of her hands.

"But *who?*" she cried in anguish. "Who would go into the jungle to look for retarded children? The war . . . " She could not go on.

"Don't worry, *njonja*," the older amah said, kneading her feet. "I'll ask the captain to do it, after he has put you and the other passengers ashore in Java. If anyone can find them, he will. I'll tell him to take along a shoe for your little boy. All right?"

Sister Ursula opened her eyes and looked at the two women. For a moment hope flared, then she sank back into despair. The captain was a cruel man. He would never go to look for any children, certainly not for the sake of someone who had refused to do his bidding.

After the women had finished and covered her with fresh linen on a clean, dry litter, she tried by fervent prayer to recapture her acceptance, to re-establish the living union with Christ. But something had changed. Was it possible that the captain might go back for the children? How could she tempt him?

Money? She had none. She had nothing of any value to offer him. Nothing at all. Except the oath.

She recoiled at the thought, aghast. That was blasphemy. She could not commit blasphemy without losing all hope of eternal life. If she forsook Christ as her Saviour, denied the existence of God, her soul would be condemned to perpetual darkness and eternal torment. But what about the magic formula the Reverend Mother and Father Sebastian had advocated? She should accept their assurance that she could swear the oath with impunity as long as she annulled it with a secret thought. She desperately tried to accept it; but she was too close to the end of her life to be able to silence the small, still voice within that said: 'It is not true.' On the brink of death she could only deal in absolute truth. All she could do was plead with the blessed Virgin to intercede on her behalf. It was too late to play with words in an effort to avoid responsibility. It would be her last witness on earth; she could not depart from life with those words; she would be worse than Peter if she did that, and there would be no forgiveness. In the beginning was the Word; as it was in the beginning, so it would be in the end. For her to speak the oath would be a mortal sin. There was no doubt about that.

Then, as the women went down the steps and vanished from sight, it came to her, with heart-stopping clarity. She had prayed for a sign, here it was.

God would send the captain to save her children, at a terrible price: she would have to sacrifice her prospect of heaven and accept the darkness and utter loneliness of hell, for all eternity.

It turned the small, sunlit deck on which she lay, shaded by palms, into the garden of Gethsemane.

10

"Benji," Baradja said the next morning as Krasser appeared on the forecastle to look at the anchor, "the Sister wants to talk to you."

Krasser had been on the bridge all night; this anchorage had been tricky because of shoaling; the last thing he needed at this point was a *klatsch* with a nun.

He checked the anchor chain, told the lookout that next time he caught him crapping behind the anchor winch he'd rub his snout in it; then Baradja pointed at the nun on the stretcher and mouthed something.

He grudgingly asked, "What does she want?"

"Ask her."

The woman on the litter tried to focus her eyes on him. You did not have to be a doctor to see that she was on her way out: her eyes had a feverish look, her face was pale and waxlike, her wispy hair soaked with perspiration.

"I would . . . like to talk to you . . . in private, captain . . . "
The words were soft; it was visibly a great effort for her to speak.

He said gruffly, "All right, girls. Clear out." To the lookout he said, *"Klootzak, flikker op."* Then he was alone with the nun. "All right, what is it?"

"I want to . . . swear the oath . . . "

He had looked forward to slumping in his deck chair, enjoying a cool drink. But the woman looked as if she meant it, so he grunted, "I'll get the Bible," and turned to go. Then she mumbled something. "What was that?"

"I'll do it . . . on one condition . . . " Her breath came in gasps; she looked as if she were dying right now.

"What's that?"

"After . . . you've taken . . . your ship to Java . . ."

"Then what?"

"You . . . you go back . . . to find my children . . . "

"Your what?"

"My retarded . . . Dyak children . . . in the Mission . . . "

Her eyes stopped him from saying what came naturally; he made an effort and asked, "Who gave you that crazy idea, lady?"

"One of your . . . nurses . . . "

He shook his head. "Sorry, Sister, you let them slip one over on you. They're as stupid as they come. Those two are the only Dyak dumb blondes in captivity."

The look she gave him made him realize that she hadn't understood. "They're stupid, see? Their front end doesn't know that their rear end is alive. They don't even know there's a war on. They live in their own world, the world my dog lives in."

He saw he should take it easy. She was as fragile as a wounded bird. But he was not about to take advantage of a dying woman. "Let me explain. We've been lucky so far, because I've sailed this coast for thirty years and know it better than the Japs. But a week from now we'll run out of shelter. My guess is we have one chance in a hundred of reaching Java. I'll have to take that chance because I have no choice. But suppose I get this ship to Java, d'you think I'd be crazy enough to turn around and go back?"

Her eyes tried to focus on his face against the brightness of the sky. She looked so lost with her wandering mind that he continued, "Look: if I get to Java, the military will requisition this ship to ferry beer or guns or junk, but one thing is as sure as—as anything: they won't send me back to Borneo. That tart didn't know what she was talking about. They're both good for only one thing—well, nursing. Did they look after you properly?"

"How . . . much of a chance . . . you may go back?"

He frowned. Something about her mystified him. "One in a million, lady."

She whispered, "I'll take that chance . . . I'll swear the oath . . . if you promise . . . "

So that's what she was up to: like the others, she had found her way out. Even in her condition, about to meet her Maker, she wanted his promise in order to accommodate her conscience. He was about to say no; but the woman was dying. To have her back among her own people on the aft deck was better than to have her kick the bucket alone with a Chinese lookout crapping behind the anchor winch. "Okay," he said, "I'll get the Bible."

At the bottom of the stairs he was met by her priest, obviously preparing to sound off. He cut the man short. "Your nun is ready to swear the oath. You'd better tell the others to get ready to take her on. She's one sick woman."

By the time he came back with his Bible a crowd had gathered at the bottom of the stairs to the forecastle.

"You," he said to the priest. "And you," to the young man he had picked up in the mouth of the Kali Woga. "You come and witness this."

When he reached the forecastle he thought she was gone, for she lay on her litter like a corpse: eyes closed, her face exuding a sort of majesty. But when he squatted beside her she opened her eyes. "Promise," she whispered.

"Okay, I promise. Put your left hand on this Bible."

She did not move. He assumed she had had second thoughts; then the priest said behind him, "She can't, she's paralyzed."

He decided to forget about the Bible. "Repeat after me: I swear."

She closed her eyes and whispered, "I swear . . . "

"God does not exist."

"God . . . does not . . . exist . . . "

"All religion is superstition."

This time she paused so long between words that he thought she'd chickened out.

"All . . . religion . . . superstition . . . "

"I'm a liar and a hypocrite."

"I'm . . . a liar . . . a hypocrite . . . "

He rose and said, "All right, gentlemen, she's all yours." He did not stay around; he needed a drink.

Fifi was waiting for him at the top of the steps to the bridge, ears cocked, head on one side, gauging his mood. "All right, pisser," he said, "how about a kiss?"

They rubbed noses; Fifi pranced ahead of him as he waddled to the door of the cabin. There he shouted, "Let's have the deck chair and my booze! Amu, bring the fan!"

The deck chair was put up, the arm-rest extension swung out. He slumped into it with a sigh of relaxation, opened his fly, lifted his leg onto the extension and said, "Go ahead."

Amu, wreathed in *Heaven Scent,* started to wave her fan with practiced gestures. The cool breeze was bliss to his crotch. Then Baradja handed him his glass. "Good girl," he said, yawning.

In a nearby palm tree behind the bridge the mynah bird gave its wolf whistle and cawed, *"I love yew!"* He tossed back his drink, handed the glass to Baradja and dozed off.

Sister Ursula died three hours later, the nuns praying around her.

PART THREE

Ghosts

1   It should have been protected by the security of the confessional, but somehow the news leaked out: Sister Ursula had sworn the oath in exchange for the captain's promise that he would go back and look for her children. Father Sebastian said he had tried until the very last moment to convince her that God would forgive her the blasphemy, but she had died convinced that because of the oath her soul would be banished to outer darkness for all eternity.

Her body was committed to the deep that same night, Father Sebastian officiating. The ship was stopped a short way off the coast; the bier rested on the rail in the moonlight, covered with a white sheet. Captain Krasser stood at the head of the bier in his number-one uniform, eager to get it over with.

Father Sebastian's voice chanted; the land breeze rustled in the palm leaves overhead; when the religious service was over, the faces, faintly visible among the trees in the moonlight, watched the captain.

"Okay, *klootzakken*," he said.

The two Chinese sailors lifted the head of the hatch cover on which the body was lying.

"One, two, three. *Ajo lekas!*"

With a slithering sound of canvas on wood the body slipped over the side, leaving the limp white sheet dangling ghostlike in the light of the moon. There was a mutter of indignation because Krasser hadn't used the phrase 'In God's name.'

"Kwan Chan!" he said. "Let's get under way! We're too damn conspicuous this far out. I'm going to move inside Tiger Reef."

He went back to the bridge; presently the engine started to throb once more and the *Henny* nosed slowly back toward the silhouettes of the palms and mangroves on the coastline.

Well, there it was: he had done it. Now every sky-pilot on board his ship had owned up that their religion was a sham, exploitation of the gullible for their own miserable ends. This was what he had set out to prove; this was, or should be, the end of his mission in life. As much as any man had sacrificed comfort, sympathy and companionship for the sake of his God, so he had for the sake of proving that there was no God. Then why this odd sense of letdown? Why had he no feeling of triumph? Why was there no sound of trumpets, no wish to hit the booze and wave the bottle at the sky, forever empty now the Old Man and his host of freaks and usurpers were gone? It probably was because he had other things to think about. Or maybe the woman's pitiful condition had got to him; it had been like taking candy from a baby.

But as he stood scanning the sea from the platform on the port wing of his bridge and felt the rhythmic throb of the engine in the soles of his feet, it came to him. It *was* the final victory, of that there could be no doubt, but it had been a shabby way of winning it: promising a dying woman he'd do something he had no intention of doing—couldn't do, even if he wanted to, because it was impossible. He would have preferred to have been standing with one foot on the chest of a slain cardinal, the crowd of the free cheering on the bleachers and granting him the ears. But you couldn't have everything. He was lucky to have the proof for all to see, in case anyone was interested, other than midgets with alcoholic fathers.

Now he'd better get himself to the forecastle and check on that Chinese *orang* swinging the lead, or they'd pile up on Tiger Reef.

A few hours later, out on the forecastle with the bo'sun sounding the channel inland of Tiger Reef, Krasser thought he heard the engine of a boat approaching. He listened, reached up for the telephone to the bridge and ordered Kwan Chan to signal DEAD SLOW to the engine room. To his Chinese bo'sun he said, "Keep the lead going."

"Yes, *tuan*." The man, invisible in the darkness, swung the lead. It hit the water with a splash. He called, "Six fathom three!"

Krasser reached for the telephone again. "Kwan Chan, enemy approaching on the port side. Tell the passengers I want absolute silence. Children and babies must be kept quiet at all costs. Steady as you go." He put the receiver back in its waterproof housing and peered into the darkness. Tiger Reef, a vicious ridge of jagged coral just below the surface, was a deadly danger to any vessel. He was the only sailor apart from the local Dyak fishermen who dared hazard inland of it. All he could do was maintain just enough speed to keep steerage and hope for the best.

There was a scrabble at his feet: he picked up Fifi to make sure she wouldn't start barking. Now he could quite clearly hear the throbbing of a slow Diesel drawing closer. There was nothing to be seen to seaward; the moon was covered by cloud, its light too diffuse even for his night-trained eyes. It sounded like a patrol boat trolling down the coast. If it had been bound for some-where it would have barreled along; sneaking along like this at half-speed meant it was on the lookout. Dutch? Japanese? He had no idea.

The bo'sun kept the lead going but whispered the soundings rather than sang them out. A hush had fallen over the ship; the only sound was the rustle of leaves in the camouflage as the young land breeze came whirling across the water.

As the roar of the Diesel drew near, Captain Krasser picked up the phone and said, "Stop engine." Kwan Chan passed on the order through the speaking tube; Krasser could feel in his feet that the tremor of the ship's engine ceased. To his alarm, so did the sound of the Diesel.

Whoever it might be out there had stopped to watch or lis-ten. Krasser grabbed Fifi's snout and held her jaws together; the little animal began to tremble.

What the devil had made that patrol boat stop? Had they seen something? The *Henny* was lying dead in the water; they could not possibly see any movement of the camouflage along the coastline. Had they heard something? Not unless they had an underwater listening device which might have detected the slow turning over of the *Henny*'s propeller. It might be mere chance; a patrolling vessel would stop occasionally to look and listen. In that case they would move on after a few minutes.

Then he detected a faint, acrid smell and knew what had happened: the crew of the patrol boat had smelled the smoke from his stack wafted across to them by the rising land breeze. Coal smoke in the jungle could mean only one thing: a steam-ship. He had been spotted.

Peering into the darkness, he thought he discerned a shadow out to sea. The moon briefly drew a faint, quivering path across the water. Then he saw the silhouette of a ship slowly drift across the moon's reflection: a raked bow, a low fantail. A Jap-anese motor torpedo boat, probably the same one he had spot-ted two days earlier through his binoculars from his hiding place in the jungle. That one had had two launching tubes, a light cannon and an anti-aircraft gun. If it detected him it could sink him with one round of its cannon. All he had to shoot back with were six antiquated rifles.

A small warmth trickled down his chest; the damn dog was peeing with fear. Small wonder; any moment now the Japs would start nosing in and switch on their searchlight. Suddenly a crazy thought struck him. It was insane, but he was a sitting duck anyhow. With a feeling of playing Russian roulette, he let go of Fifi's snout and said, "Speak!"

The trembling little beast obediently gave a shrill yap.

"Speak!"

"Yap yap! Yap yap! Yap yap!"

The bow of the MTB swung toward them, a searchlight flashed on, an engine roared; in the halo of the searchlight a bow wave creamed to life. Cries of horror came from the passengers on deck. Krasser shouted, "Shut up!" They fell silent at once.

The searchlight swept the shoreline as the MTB came roaring in, ready to destroy the ship that lurked there. Suddenly there was a splintering crunch as the boat hit Tiger Reef at full speed. The searchlight went out; there was a blinding flash, a deafening explosion, then the billowing fireball of burning gasoline.

Krasser grabbed the telephone to the bridge and shouted, "Dead slow ahead! Steady as you go!" To Kwan Chan he said, "Keep the lead going! Call when you hit five!"

He hurried back to the bridge. The passengers cheered as he passed, but he paid no attention. He went to the wheelhouse to check the course, climbed the compass and snapped, "Take her up one point!"

"Up one point," Kwan Chan replied at the wheel.

Baradja appeared in the doorway and cooed, "Drinkies?"

"Yes," Captain Krasser said. "Good girl! Rotgut all round."

He waddled to the chartroom, opened the pencil drawer and offered Fifi a cookie from a priest. She proudly refused until it came from an atheist.

2   To Krasser the business with the MTB had been no more than a stroke of good fortune. Had the *Henny* not found herself behind the invisible ramparts of Tiger Reef, the Jap would have sunk her. To call it a miracle was laughable; yet this was what his passengers were doing, as he discovered the morning after when they lay at anchor for the day in Sappo Lidi cove.

He was sitting in the chartroom listening to the radio when Baradja came in with the morning eye-opener. "Put out that anti-mosquito incense," he said. "If there are any Japs around they'll smell the stench a mile off."

Baradja said, "I'm not burning any mosquito coils."

"Then who is?"

"Some of the people on deck. Peanuts?"

Krasser went out onto the bridge, sniffed, climbed onto the platform and saw on the forecastle a small group of passengers huddled together in a circle, on their knees. He slid down the stairs, waddled through the jungle to the steps to the forecastle, appeared in their midst and asked gruffly, "What the hell is going on here?"

132

The worshippers looked up; in the center of their circle a glowing mosquito coil smoked on a saucer.

Krasser said, "Douse that stuff! And don't let me catch you burning it again. That scent can be picked up a mile away! What's more, I told you I don't want any passengers hanging around on this fo'c'sle! Get the hell out of here."

They looked at him with a glint of defiance in their eyes; but one of them squeezed the glowing spark between his finger and thumb and squealed with pain.

"Throw it overboard!" Krasser said. The man obeyed. Then Krasser singled out the Catholic priest. "You come with me, I want a word with you."

The priest rose reluctantly and followed him across the crowded deck to a corner under the bridge, where they were out of earshot.

"What do you mean," Krasser asked, "holding a church service on the fo'c'sle? You swore an oath you'd lay off that stuff. You'd better stick to it, friend, or I'll toss you back into the jungle."

The priest eyed him defiantly. "It was a memorial service for Sister Ursula. A service of thanks for her intercession. She saved our lives."

"*She* saved your lives?"

"By blowing up the gunboat. That was a miracle if ever I saw one."

"Boy," Krasser said, shaking his head, "talk about superstition! If you want to thank anyone after that miracle, friend, thank my dog."

The priest stalked off, leaving Krasser in a quandary. Stamp out religious exercises altogether, or just enforce a ban on mosquito coils? Maybe it was best to allow them some mumbo-jumbo. He'd rather they went to their deaths on their knees praying to a dead nun than hanging in the rigging, screaming, as the Japanese gunners picked them off.

So, let them pray to their private deity. He was going to have a drink.

3   To Herman Winsum, who witnessed it all as from a private perch in this garden of folly, it was a fascinating process.

First, in spite of the captain's stern disapproval, daily memorial services for Sister Ursula were held, then prayer sessions three times a day. The captain had put the forecastle out of bounds, so the worshippers gathered at the bottom of the steps that led to it.

It was like a history of Christianity speeded up ten thousand times; the Dark Ages were reached when Mr. Faber—who, maybe because of his macabre profession, had a realistic view of human gullibility—started to barter, for cigarettes, small pieces of what he said was Sister Ursula's blood-stained habit, the one in which she had arrived and which had been exchanged for a clean one by the nuns. Father Sebastian and the Reverend Mother, who must have been aware of the transactions, turned a blind eye. Mr. Faber did a brisk trade; after a few days everyone on board except the children had a snippet of the saint's garment tucked away somewhere as a sort of holy rabbit's foot. The rationale for this idolatry was that Sister Ursula had sacrificed the future of her soul in exchange for the captain's promise to go back to Borneo and look for her children, consequently she had a vested interest in keeping him alive and able to live up to his part of the bargain. Therefore the ship was now protected by a guardian angel: the saintly nun, floating overhead like a spiritual albatross.

Herman could afford to observe all this with detached interest; Zandstra, as a minister whose flock was involved in these Papist dealings, had a problem. Ultimately, true to the adage 'If you can't lick 'em, join 'em,' he shrugged it off, saying, "In adversity, all roads lead to God."

The source of Herman's detachment was guilt. He was haunted by the image of the little cherub with the empty eyesockets, by Mr. Palstra's bifocals mirroring the sun. Here he was, sole survivor of forty-eight men who had trudged to their death in the mountains; it was as if the knowledge that he was to blame for their fate prevented him from feeling wholly alive. He was aware of their presence all the time.

What was to become of him? What would he do, if the *Henny* ever arrived in Java? Would he simply pick up life at the point where the hotel manager had burst into the conference room? Join the press corps? Be a war correspondent? And what about Mrs. Bohm? Some primitive part of him, an extrasensory perception, told him she was dead too. He was all alone with forty-seven secret sharers watching his every move, reading his every thought.

Occasionally he felt the pull to join them. There were moments when he was suddenly tempted to slip through the shrubs of the camouflage and plunge into the sea. What held him back was the picture of submarine life, not as painted by Odilon Redon, but by Hieronymus Bosch: soft, sucking mouths of bug-eyed fish glued to his flesh, nibbling on the lips that Josephine Bohm had kissed, eating the eyes that had beheld such beauty and such horror.

He felt no urge to live. It was of no interest to him whether he would eventually reach Java or not. Consequently he was immune to the spell of the saintly nun. He could not accept that her spirit was now protecting the ship. The whole concept was thoroughly unspiritual: she had struck a bargain with the captain and would make damn sure that he lived up to his end of it.

That evening he found an unexpected diversion in Lieutenant Hin, still sweating it out in the bo'sun's locker on the aft deck, now with a Rasputin beard instead of the stubble of the Prisoner of Zenda. The business with the Japanese gunboat unexpectedly caused Hin to capitulate. Up to now he had been swearing country-club oaths that he would see little Krasser garroted, shot, electrocuted or gassed, even if he had to do it himself; now, suddenly, he said: "Winsum, would you do me a favor? Go and see the dwarf and tell him I'd like to have a word with him. I want to tender my apologies."

"Excuse me?"

"I'll explain it to you, if you'll keep it to yourself. I have an offer to make to him: once we get to Java, I'm prepared to declare that I officially requisitioned his ship in behalf of Her Majesty and ordered him to sail down the coast to pick up survivors. I still want to see the little bastard drawn and quartered eventually; but first I want him to honor his promise to that woman. I intend to be on his back until he does. After that, it will be my pleasure to shoot him, personally."

So, willy-nilly, Herman became the emissary of the repentant sinner in the paint locker to the wrathful dwarf on the bridge. He climbed the steps to the bridge with a sense of daring. It was his first visit; when he arrived he didn't know where to go. Should he knock on one of the closed doors? He made his way toward the front of the bridge and looked into the wheelhouse. There seemed to be no one there, but then a singsong voice asked, "Yes, please?" and someone emerged from a dark corner: the smiling Chinese mate.

"I'd like a word with the captain, if I may."

"Captain busy. Very sorry."

"It's of some urgency. Would you please tell him I *must* see him? I won't take up much of his time."

The Chinese stepped into the sunlight, gave him a snakelike look without letting up on his smile, went to one of the closed doors on the bridge and knocked. Someone answered, he slipped inside. After a few moments he reappeared and said, "Captain will see you."

In response to his inviting gesture, Herman stepped over a high threshold into almost total darkness. The first thing he noticed was a smell he remembered from the native kampong at Banjermasin; then his eyes got used to the darkness and he discerned the shapes of two half-naked women who were cutting up a large sheet of paper on a table under a porthole, probably a dress pattern. The captain, in singlet and rumpled white pants, peered at him from an armchair, little legs stretched out, barely reaching the edge of the seat.

"What do you want?"

"I—er—I have a message from Lieutenant Hin, captain."

"Who?"

"Hin, sir. The one in the paint locker." He glanced around the cabin and noticed, beside the door, a miniature harmonium with a keyboard so reduced that it seemed to have been made for only one hand. As far as he could make out in the murk, there was a lot of junk crammed into the cabin: a tallboy, a buffet, a sort of altar on which a gilded idol with a pixie hat sat airing its arms like a cormorant drying its wings.

"Well?" the captain snarled. "What has he got to say?"

Herman explained his mission; as he was doing so, the mynah bird descended on the table with a flutter of wings, shrieked,

"I love yew!" and squirted a white jet onto the women's paper pattern, setting them squealing. The captain yelled, "Pack it up!" His dog rolled onto its back and licked its nose. The captain said, "If you piss, you slut, I'll rip everything off: ears, tail, legs; you'll end up as a cylinder!" He reached for a bottle and a glass, poured himself a drink, put the bottle between his short thighs, tossed back his drink and poured another. Then he called, "Kwan Chan!"

The door opened and the Chinese mate came in, smiling. "Yes, *tuan?*"

"Let the prisoner out of the locker."

"Very well, *tuan.*"

"Anything else?"

Herman realized he was being addressed. "No, er, thank you. . . . "

"All right, then. Get out."

It was a relief to step back into the sunlight.

4   After the *klootzak* had left, Captain Krasser stared at the closed door. It was not hard to see what they were after. The lieutenant, who had thought a lot of that nun, wanted to make sure he kept his promise. What baffled him was the blithe conviction the man must share with the rest of the passengers that they would actually arrive in Java. It should be obvious even to a fool that they didn't have a chance, yet all of them behaved as if they were on a peacetime cruise, their arrival a foregone conclusion. Well, at least superstition had overcome the dogfood.

It was getting hot in the cabin and the women were bickering, so he picked up his bottle and glass and went out onto the bridge. First, he climbed onto the platform and scanned the horizon; then, satisfied there was nothing to be seen, he put up a deck chair to enjoy his drink in peace and slumped back with a sigh. Then Fifi started to whine beside him. Grumbling, he hoisted himself back to his feet, waddled to the chartroom, climbed onto the stool, rummaged in the pencil drawer, brought out a biscuit and took it back to the chair. Fifi rose expectantly on her haunches, sly old eyes ready to squint at the cookie on her nose. "All right," he said. "This cookie is from a priest."

Fifi, the biscuit on her nose, teetering because of her squint, panted with anticipation. "A *priest*," he said. "This is a *priest's* cookie." When Fifi seemed about to keel over, he relented. "All right, it's from an *atheist!*"

She tossed the biscuit into the air, but for the first time in her life failed to catch it. It fell on the deck and rolled away; Fifi, frozen with fright, sat staring at something behind him. He whipped around, thinking the Chinese bastard was about to plunge a dagger into his back, but the bridge was empty. All doors were closed, there wasn't a soul in sight. The dog sat bolt upright, bug-eyed with fright, neck hair bristling; around her haunches a puddle grew on the deck.

"What the hell is the matter with you?"

Fifi growled, then slowly pivoted on her haunches as if her eyes were following something which moved from the stairs to the chartroom. Then she lost sight of whatever it was and rolled on her back, licking her nose.

Her performance had been so convincing that Krasser lowered himself out of the deck chair and went to have a look in the chartroom. Nothing. She must have seen a mud wasp.

He returned to his chair; Fifi was abjectly licking her urine off the deck. "If you do that again," he said, "you go straight into Nanking pie. Scram!"

Fifi slunk off. He sat for a while, then he went back into the chartroom, turned on the old radio receiver and gave it a slap to make it work. The loudspeaker scratchily emitted a twitter of Morse signals. He could not read them: they were scrambled, whether in Dutch, English or Japanese. He wished he knew what they meant. On the one hand, the more confusion there was of ships chasing one another the better, but he didn't want to run still out of range of the news broadcasts of Radio Batavia; they probably wouldn't tell the truth about what was going on anyhow. Had Celebes been occupied by the Japanese? Had they landed in Java? Was Sumatra still in the hands of the Dutch? That was of vital importance, for tomorrow he would have to make his decision: either cross from Pulu Laut directly to Java, or continue to crawl along the coast to Karimata Strait and cross to Billiton and Sumatra. Crossing the Java Sea would take longer, but there was likely to be less traffic than in Karimata Strait, the busiest seaway in the Dutch East Indies. The idea of crossing open water at all gave him the creeps. Not just because of the Japs; he was a coaster captain, he had never lost sight of land for thirty years.

He climbed onto the stool, then onto the table, pulled the general chart of the Malay Archipelago out of the overhead rack, unrolled it and pondered the alternatives. As he stood looking at the chart, a little red louse set out from Balik Papan on a southerly course. He went to squash it; then, on an impulse, he waited to see where it would go.

The louse walked down the coast of Borneo to Pulu Laut, hesitated, turned starboard and went on following the coast to Pulu Maja. There it hesitated again, turned port and crossed Karimata Strait to Billiton. From Billiton it sailed across to Banka, followed the coast of Sumatra to Sunda Strait and set out into the Indian Ocean. It sailed on and on, on a steady course, full speed; then it dropped off the table.

"Benji?"

Baradja was leaning in the doorway, smoking a cigarette.

"What do you want?"

She inhaled, held the smoke in her lungs, exhaled and said, "The nun taught an idiot Dyak child how to lace a shoe. It took her four months. Isn't that something? For a white woman?"

"Bugger off," he said. "I'm listening to the radio."

She shrugged and left. The Morse signals were overlapping each other now with twittering urgency.

He turned off the radio, disgusted with Benjamin Krasser, legendary atheist, swayed by the wanderings of a louse.

5

Ten days later the *Henny* crossed Karimata Strait: a tiny island broken away from the shore, freshly refurbished with palms and greenery. She sailed at a speed of six knots, in plain view of any destroyer, battleship, submarine or plane that might happen by. None did.

At first it was surprising, then amazing; toward the end of the bright, cloudless day it had become miraculous. Even though the radio twittered like an aviary, not a ship, not a plane, not a soul was in sight on the shimmering expanse of sunlit sea. The only life in its sparkle and dazzle was the wheezing old ship plodding across, lurching and rolling, loaded with swaying palms, squeaky mangroves and seasick children. The smell of incense from the forecastle was stifling.

When night fell after a day with only the playful dolphins and wave-hopping flying fish for company, a feeling of awe settled over the ship, even over those too stupid to realize the full extent of the danger they had run. Captain Krasser was not about to knuckle under to the general belief in the miraculous protection

142

of a guardian angel. There must be a rational explanation for the fact that, in the midst of an invasion, the Strait was stripped of all traffic while the radio went berserk in indecipherable code. If he had been born with normal legs and not schooled himself for thirty years in the rationality of atheism, he would have gone down on his knees like the rest of them to offer a prayer of thanks to St. Ursula.

When they sighted the island of Billiton at dawn, the stench of incense could be cut with a knife and the mumbled prayers made the ship sound like a beehive. There *had* to be a rational explanation for the busiest strait in the Far East to have been devoid of human life that day. He received no answer, for that night the radio fell silent.

The *Henny* started to slink down the coast of Sumatra as she had the coast of Borneo: ghosting along the edge of the jungle at dead of night, holing up each day in a cove or a river's mouth. Krasser began to pick up Radio Batavia, and after a week the miracle was explained: the day the *Henny* had crossed Karimata Strait, the Japanese and Allied navies had met in battle in the Java Sea. Although Radio Batavia tried to keep up the pretense of continuous resistance to the invader, it was obvious even from its doctored news that the Allied Navy had been destroyed, that Java had fallen, and with it the Dutch East Indies. It meant that by the time the *Henny* got to Java she would be sailing straight into the arms of the Japanese.

Krasser labored for many hours on his stool at the chart table, poring over charts, doing sums on bits of paper, looking up mileages in distance tables and weather predictions on the meteorological chart of the Indian Ocean. In the end, he resigned himself to the fact that the nearest port of call free of Japs was Onslow, Australia.

To head for Australia was crazy. Apart from the fact that his rickety old bucket had no business in the Indian Ocean, it would mean six days and nights on open water in plain view of any patrolling vessel or aircraft. But the alternative was hibernating somewhere in the Sumatra jungle for the duration with fifty-odd passengers and children on board. That was out of the question. He had no choice but to hit the ocean.

First of all, however, he had to get this ship through Sunda Strait, and Sumatra proved no easy going. He knew the coast of Borneo like the back of his hand. Here he had to keep the lead going continuously and spend half his time scrutinizing charts by bad light, trying to work out where the hell he was. He managed to avoid the shoals and bars that were marked; but any moment he expected the telltale crunch of some uncharted Tiger Reef known only to the local fishermen. It was enough to give a man an ulcer, but at least it kept his mind off the Japs and their spies ashore, of which by now there must be whole tribes, peering from the jungle or cooling their feet sitting on rocks in a river's mouth, wondering whether they did indeed see what they thought they saw: a little island floating by. He hoped they'd react the way Fifi had to the mud wasp: wet their sarongs and lope back into the jungle.

On the eve of the fifth night he approached a reef that looked, on the chart, like the plan for a rock garden. He started to work out a course through it, then decided the lesser of two evils would be to give it a wide berth and join the coast again after he had left it behind. It meant hazarding into the open, but so be it. He was about to give the order to change course when the ship heeled over slightly in the lazy swell, setting his pencil rolling on the chart. He hunted it down before it fell to the floor; then he noticed it was aligned exactly with the tentative course he had drawn through the maze of the reef. He picked it up, put it on the center of the chart, turned to go; he had one foot off the stool when the ship heeled again, lazily. He heard the pencil roll, it made him turn around: the pencil was back in the same place, on the line he had drawn through the reef. It was crazy, it would mean working his butt off, darting from chart to compass to telephone and back, but he decided to hazard the reef.

He was deep inside the maze when the lookout reported

engine noise, three points off the port bow. He instantly stopped his own engine and sent Kwan Chan to order the passengers to maintain absolute silence. There was a slight sea breeze, so the smoke of their stack was blown inland; this time no one to seaward would smell them. And they were so close to the coast now that they couldn't be seen either.

It was a small destroyer, Japanese no doubt. It came sauntering past at half-speed, occasionally sweeping the shore with its searchlight. Everyone on deck and on the bridge held their breath as they watched its silhouette ghost by. When the destroyer's searchlight flashed on again to sweep the shore it was well past them.

Relieved and weary, Krasser worked his way through the rest of the maze of rocks and reefs. He had had narrow escapes before and never indulged in idle speculation as to what would have happened had he steered just a little higher, or left port a little later. This time, however, he knew for certain that the destroyer would have run straight into the *Henny* had he taken the course around the reef.

If Fifi hadn't gone in for her mud-wasp pantomime, he wouldn't have given it a thought; now he was faced with the fact that he had reversed his decision to take the seaward course only because of the damn pencil. Crazy to assume that a spectral intelligence could guide the rolling of a pencil, but there it was.

Fifi peered over the threshold, her head on one side, a devout look in her sly old eyes. "The hell with you," he cried. "Go and get your cookies from cook! Go piss your way to Australia in the galley!"

The dog disappeared in the pale light of the dawn.

Australia. They would never make it. They would drop right off the edge if he took this leaking old bucket out into the Indian Ocean.

Then he remembered the red louse. It had headed south into the open after Sunda Strait and dropped right off the edge.

Boy, he was as superstitious as the rest of them! Next thing you knew, the hair in the nape of his neck would bristle, like Fifi seeing a ghost. The damned nun had reduced his once proud and independent mind to that of a dog.

6 The *Henny*'s luck held. The fact that they managed to sneak down the coast of Sumatra and through Sunda Strait unnoticed was due to Krasser's wizardry; the passengers attributed it to St. Ursula. While the ship edged along the jungle under cover of darkness and hid during the daytime in coves and river mouths, everybody prayed to the *Henny*'s guardian angel.

Once they left the coast behind, the camouflage was discarded. First to go were the jungle creepers draped around the derricks, the shrouds and the rail; they were torn down and dumped overboard. As they slowly sank below the surface in the wake of the ship, they looked like wreaths thrown out after a funeral. Then the mangroves were disentangled from the winches, the stairs to the forecastle and the machinery on the aft deck and ditched; they sank at once. Finally the palms, slender and naked, slowly toppled and dived head first into the sea.

Herman watched it happen with mixed feelings. To see the

last of the jungle disappear down the ephemeral ship's wake gave him the sensation of awakening in a new reality. Then a voice beside him said, "Well, good riddance!"

It was Zandstra, looking somehow victorious. "Glad all that junk is gone! Now, maybe we can start leading a normal life!"

Herman didn't know what the man meant, so he said nothing and strolled away, down the bare deck, which suddenly seemed much smaller. On the poop, he leaned over the rail and gazed at the distant horizon. Strange, this sensation of awakening. The camouflage had not been gone for more than an hour; already it seemed as if the past had not really happened. The thought struck him that probably he could never make anyone who hadn't shared the experience believe the story: *'The captain disguised the ship as an island and we managed, with a few hair-raising narrow escapes, to crawl along the edge of the jungle unnoticed.'* But somehow that was not the true story.

He stood gazing out over the sea, wondering what the spell had been that now seemed removed from him, when Faber the mortician joined him. "Well, isn't this a relief?"

"I'm not sure," Herman said, scanning the empty horizon. "The Japs are somewhere out there. We're a lot more visible now than we were before."

Faber patted his shoulder patronizingly. "Don't be gloomy, young friend. The worst is over." It was probably what the man used to say to his customers' next of kin.

Faber strolled away, hands behind his back, at the tempo of a constitutional. Lots of people were doing constitutionals on deck now, Herman noticed—marching to and fro, limbering up, doing knee-bends and push-ups. Was he the one who was crazy? Was the danger to a naked ship, all alone on the ocean in broad daylight, not infinitely greater than that to a little island ghosting along the coast at dead of night, indistinguishable from the jungle?

As the day went on he realized that everybody seemed to be

in tacit agreement that the story of what had occurred on board the *Henny* should be edited. He was drawn into a conversation between Zandstra and the Catholic priest and heard Father Sebastian say, "It was pretty rough on us spiritual leaders, but I can see why the captain had to assert his authority the way he did. Discipline on board ship might well have disintegrated otherwise."

Within hours after the discarding of the camouflage, the consensus of opinion seemed to be that Captain Krasser was a rough diamond who had risked his life and his ship to save his fellow countrymen from certain death. The little old salt's efforts to pamper them after the hardships they had gone through had been touching: improvised Chinese dinners, *bami, nasi-goreng.* Of course, experienced mariner as he was, he had refused to tolerate any authority other than his own. But what an original way of going about it! How wise and sensitive on the part of the clergy to recognize the need for it and accept it gracefully! If anyone deserved a medal from Her Majesty it was stout-hearted Captain Krasser, searfaring hero in the best national tradition, chip off the old block.

What surprised Herman was that this change of heart seemed to be accompanied by the peremptory dismissal of Sister Ursula as their patron saint. No more prayer sessions near the forecastle, no more offerings of incense; from the snippets of conversation he overheard, it became clear that while the captain was being promoted to National Hero, Sister Ursula was being cut down to size. Simple-minded old dear; how generous of the captain to have played along with her! Of course, no one in his senses would hold a man to a promise impossible to fulfill. What was more, her pathetic retarded children must long since have vanished in the jungle and were probably dead anyhow.

Even Hin, despite his bloodthirsty soliloquies in the paint locker, seemed to have dropped the role of executor of Sister Ursula's last will. He turned out to be popular with the ladies because of an unexpected talent: he was a virtuoso on the mouth organ. Some child had brought one on board; Hin had heard him tootle on it, asked if he might borrow it for a moment and given vent to a rendition of a *Toccata* by Bach that would have brought Paganini to his knees. After this conspicuous beginning he proceeded to dazzle the ladies with imitations of gypsy violinists, departing locomotives and a typewriter, all this on a two-dollar harmonica decorated with gnomes. His musical prowess drew women as the scent of an exotic flower draws bees. Given these heady circumstances, it must be difficult to maintain his dedication to a fallen saint. Clearly, Captain Krasser had been relieved of his promise by common consent; the passengers were planning instead to petition Her Majesty to grant him a knighthood as a reward for their soon-to-be legendary rescue.

Herman realized that together with the vines and rustling palms of their camouflage the ghosts that had haunted their floating little wilderness had vanished. While the laboring propeller pushed them slowly closer to the civilized world, the horrors they had lived through were left behind. After three days, nothing remained but an exciting tale with which to edify their children and stultify their grandchildren. Herman managed to hold out longer than the others for each time he gazed at the wake of the ship, two lines of foam converging on the far horizon, he saw the men of Rauwatta staring at him, empty-eyed, in a mute plea for remembrance. But they too became fainter and fainter while Lieutenant Hin played *The Flight of the Bumble Bee,* the women giggled and swooned, the Reverend Zandstra started his memoirs, Mr. Faber opened betting on their date of arrival in Australia and Mrs. de Winter started a campaign to cover the breasts of the captain's ladies before they reached civilization. The nuns sang touching little songs about hanging Albigensians for the sake of Christ; Father Sebastian took his siesta on number-one hatch, stretched out in his cassock like the effigy of a bishop on a medieval tomb.

As Herman turned away from the past he started to muse, tentatively, on the future. It first presented itself in a nebulous vision as he lay open-eyed under the night sky: Josephine Bohm undressing among the stars. It was a vision of such surging vitality and abundant promise that he suddenly felt certain she was alive after all.

Bemused by a sense of betrayal, he tried to plan a dream as he closed his eyes to sleep that night: Josie and he alone, nude, on a white sandy beach, in a world at peace.

Instead, he dreamed he was standing on the steps to the bridge, wanting to speak to Captain Krasser, but being forced to wait as Sister Ursula came down the stairs. She was smoking a pipe which left the sweet scent of the kampong after she passed.

7 The only one who continued to believe in Sister Ursula's presence on board the *Henny* was Fifi, the ship's dog. Before Krasser became aware of this, a few things happened that seemed quite normal in hindsight but raised his eyebrows when they occurred.

To start with, there was the business with the cable of number-one winch. It was used to hoist the loading boom which picked up the palm trees and dumped them over the side. The passengers were kept at a distance during the operation, but Krasser himself roamed freely under the sweep of the boom, directing which trees to pick up, as he did not want his Chinese morons to knock down ventilators or sideswipe the wheelhouse with a palm tree. When the operation was completed and the boom safely lowered onto its rest, the donkeyman—petty officer of the engine-room crew—came with his bucket and brush to grease the cable.

Krasser was interfering with Amu in a corner of the chartroom when the donkeyman called from below, "*Tuan! Tuan!* Look!"

Cursing, he arranged his clothing, went to the bridge and climbed onto the platform to look. The donkeyman stood by number-one winch, holding up the frayed end of the steel cable. "*Tuan!* It was *broken!*"

So it was. Not the cable, but the clamp that secured the end of it to the drum of the winch. On inspection, the break turned out to be of long standing. There was no logical explanation of how the cable could have been worked for hours without the heavy loading boom crashing down. The captain, who had waddled to and fro underneath it, should by human reckoning have been mashed to pulp. Krasser shrugged his shoulders and discounted the instance as one of the many lucky breaks a sailor must have if he is to live in maturity in his profession.

The second incident was, in hindsight, just another stroke of luck. One night while leaning over the rail of the bridge, Krasser received a visit from the mynah bird, which, after the dumping of the camouflage, showed an increased need for human company. It came fluttering out of the cabin, evicted by the girls for some reason, and settled on the rail next to him. After telling him in its cretinous voice that it loved him, it gave its wolf whistle. Not once, but continuously. Krasser said, "Shut up!" but the bird, head on one side, beady eye staring at the starboard ventilator, whistled on and on as if it were staking out its territory against an intruder. If Krasser had not been standing where he stood, and if the mynah bird had not settled right next to him, the intruder challenging the bird's territory would never have been heard by him. Now he discerned between the mynah bird's wolf whistles a rhythmic squeak coming from the ventilator. It was so faint that he had to listen sharply to pick it up among the hissings and puffings and stampings from the engine room channeled by the ventilator. After a while he went to investigate.

He descended into the hot hellhole with its smell of grease and used steam and its deafening racket of pistons, and found it impossible to locate the squeak because of the deafening level of noise. So he took his Chinese chief engineer up to the bridge and made him listen to the ventilator; both decided that something was wrong; but what?

They went back below and proceeded to check all joints, elbows and bearings of the engine individually. Finally they located the trouble: one of the bearings of the propeller axle had run dry and was overheating, a problem impossible to detect because the vent of the oiling cup was clogged shut, a circumstance no one could spot by sight. In another hour the bearing would have burned out, jamming the axle and grinding the engine to a halt. The chief would have been unable to repair it temporarily with a side of bacon, as he had done on previous occasions, because there were no sides of bacon left, only cans of *Fido's Delight.*

Krasser returned to the bridge in a thoughtful mood, gave the mynah bird a handful of peanuts and considered the implications of the incident. To find himself with a dead engine drifting in the Indian Ocean was a circumstance he did not care to contemplate. Whatever the reason, they were in a lucky streak.

A few days later Fifi, sound asleep by his chair on the bridge, rose on her haunches, neck hair bristling, and once more followed with popping eyes the passage of an invisible presence from the stairs to the chartroom, exactly the same performance she had given off the coast of Sumatra. The apparition must be more familiar to her by now, for no puddle appeared this time. But what the devil did she see?

There were no mud wasps this far out; even so, Krasser could not resist looking into the chartroom to check if there might be, after all, some other insect trapped in there. As he stood in the doorway looking around, his attention was caught by a faint voice saying, *"Attention all shipping attention all shipping."*

It was the radio. He turned up the volume; the voice went on, difficult to hear because of static. *"This is a one-time warning repeat one-time warning breaking radio silence. Japanese destroyers patrolling Indian Ocean in the area east of 110, west of 130, south of 10, and north of 30. All shipping bound for Australia is urgently advised to avoid this area until further notice. End of message."* The radio resumed its empty crackling and hissing.

He stared at it, then moved quickly to the chart table. He'd have to change course at once to due south—but this ruled out Onslow as a landfall. He would have to continue on his new course down to latitude 30. The first landfall after that was Perth.

It meant another week before they made port, but it was better than being picked off by a Jap destroyer while trundling on to Onslow. What if he hadn't happened to enter the chart-room just as the message was being broadcast? The volume of the radio had been turned too low to be heard on the bridge. Kwan Chan must have fiddled with it during his watch, spun the dial to pick up a signal and, hearing nothing, failed to turn off the receiver. Krasser called him on the mat for it; of course the sly bastard denied having touched the radio. They all lied like soothsayers when faced with incriminating evidence. Somebody must have left that radio on, though, and it could only have been Kwan Chan. Be that as it may: lucky once more.

The captain might be aware of their extraordinary good fortune, but the passengers appeared totally unconcerned, as if all danger were past. The children played happily on the decks, the women sunbathed and gossiped, the men sat in groups in the shade and played cards or discussed the future, which obviously did not include a sinking ship, fire at sea, drowning people trying to claw their way into overcrowded boats and being beaten off with oars. These visions haunted Krasser; he was forever scanning the horizon, troubled and uneasy.

Even the dogfood issue was raised again—this time because the portions had been reduced so as to eke out their stores another week. Shouldn't the men get more than the women? Couldn't the captain come up with something else to eat? Wasn't there a store of rolled oats on board meant for an emergency, as Mr. Faber maintained was the case on all ships certified by the government? What about some hot cereal to supplement their rations? The captain regarded the messenger somberly; humanity had seemed to have more dignity when his passengers still worshipped the nun.

As the days slowly crawled by, Krasser became more ill at ease. Something was in the air. Someone was observing the ship. A plane? No engine could be heard, no speck showed in the sky. A submarine? There was nothing to be seen, yet the sixth sense of the born sailor kept him on the bridge at all hours, scanning the oily, somnolent sea.

On the evening of the fifth day, as night was falling, he thought he detected a glint on the horizon. To Krasser it suggested the reflection of the setting sun in a window of the wheelhouse of a rolling ship. Darkness was settling fast; he strained his eyes until he could see no longer. His sixth sense was almost in a state of panic when, ten minutes later, all navigation lights were turned on and a woman's voice called, "Benji! Drinkies!"

"Stupid whore!" He made a dash for the switch in the chartroom; before he got to it a searchlight flashed on over starboard and a bullhorn bellowed, "Good show, captain! I nearly pranged you there! What's your cargo, where are you bound?"

With shaky knees Krasser stumbled to the rail, climbed onto the platform and answered through his megaphone, "Bound for Perth with fifty-four passengers! Who are you?"

"Australian frigate H.M.S. Brisbane!" the bullhorn bellowed back. *"Stop your engine! I'm boarding!"*

Within minutes a motor launch crammed with naval ratings came foaming into the searchlight's path. Kwan Chan threw out the rope ladder; a lieutenant commander of the Royal Australian Navy came clambering on board, dressed in white shorts, white knee-stockings, short-sleeved shirt with tabs and tennis shoes. "Hello there," he said, shaking Krasser by the hand after a moment's surprise at his size. "Pretty nippy of you, captain, to light up the second you heard me! One minute later and I would have opened fire!"

"Why?"

"Surely you know that you're supposed to show running lights below latitude thirty? I took you to be a Jap."

Kwan Chan joined them with the jug and the glasses; the officer tossed back his drink, blew out his cheeks, eyes bulging, then slowly let out the air and said, "Crikey! What do you call *this?*"

Krasser explained the composition of his house brand; they shared a few more before the Australian departed. H.M.S. *Brisbane* would escort the *Henny* until another warship came to take over and guide her in. The commander loved the idea of a Dutch coaster disguising itself as an island and smuggling out fifty survivors under the very noses of the Japs. "Good show, captain! When I get to Fremantle, I'll tell them about you! What shape are your passengers in?"

Krasser said they were doing fine, and that he hoped somebody would take them off his hands as soon as possible.

The commander grinned. "Don't worry, old man. The ladies of the St. John's Ambulance Brigade will have a field day with them. Once they're ashore their feet will never touch the ground."

Later that night, with Kwan Chan at the wheel trailing the taillight of the frigate, Krasser called Baradja to task and raked her over the coals. It might have cost them all their lives, her lighting up the whole ship. Baradja protested that she had only wanted to turn on the chartroom light, and couldn't understand how she had mixed up the switches.

"But what the hell were you serving drinks for in the middle of a watch? That's an absolute taboo!"

"*You* called for them, Benji! You called for them yourself!"

"I did what!"

"You called: 'Baradja! Bring the drinkies!'"

"You're a mixed-up, stupid broad," Krasser said, "a menace to the ship. I'll ditch you in Australia."

Baradja tossed her hair and said haughtily, "*Sudah!* Me and Amu had already decided: we're leaving. We're going to be nurses."

Krasser laughed himself sick at the idea of two Dyak whores trying to infiltrate the St. John's Ambulance Brigade. But his laughter was strained; the spook stuff was finally getting to him. Who had held the loose end of the cable to the winch after the clamp broke? Who had made the mynah bird respond to the squeak of the overheating axle bearing? Who had Fifi seen walk into the chartroom, causing him to look in there in time to catch the radio alert about Japanese raiders? Whose voice had Baradja mistaken for his when she thought she heard him call for drinks, and who had guided her stupid hand to switch on the navigation lights in the nick of time to prevent their being sunk by the Australian commander?

Krasser had no quarrel with the notion that something might linger on for a while after a person died. That had nothing to do with religion but with *guna-guna,* of which he had witnessed too many instances these last thirty years to dismiss it out of hand. So the nun, or part of the nun, lingered on and haunted his ship. She lived in a different dimension now where she could see things before they happened and trigger reflexes in simple-minded Dyak women. But there could only be one reason why she lingered: she wanted to make sure he kept his promise.

Obviously she was trying to intimidate him by getting him so scared and jumpy that he'd fall over himself to get back to Borneo. But she could not alter the fact that in Australia his ship would be requisitioned and assigned to wartime duty, and they sure as hell would not send him to Borneo. He had tried to explain that to her while she was still alive; maybe if he could have a quiet chat with her ghost he could get it through to her this time. She was barking up the wrong tree: it was not he who should go back, but she. Let her go and scare the sarongs off anyone who wanted to harm her kids—now, *there* was a sensible mission.

He wondered whether ghosts read minds and decided to say it out loud: in a corner of the platform on the bridge, out of earshot of the wheelhouse. He stood, green ghost himself in the glow of the starboard navigation light, and said, keeping his voice low, "Come on, Sister. Be sensible, woman. Don't flog your . . . Don't get hung up on something that's impossible. This ship will never go back to Borneo while there's a war on, they simply won't allow it. They'll assign her to carry junk and booze up and down the coast of Australia; maybe a hop to Tasmania once in a while. Borneo? Forget it. Thanks for all you did for this ship and for yours truly, if it was indeed you; now be sensible and scoot over to Borneo yourself. Go back to your kids, Sister. You can protect them better than anyone alive, if you see what I mean. Just picture it: a bunch of Japs or Dyaks trying to harm your kids. All you need do is go bump in the night, or roll a pencil on their chart, or scare their dog the way you did mine. You know the natives after your years in the jungle; they're scared of their own shadows. So go on, fly home and give them a good jolt! Scare the daylights out of them and they'll start to spoil your kids, give 'em food, dollies, bunny rabbits. One good scare, and they'll turn your kids into little gods. Come on, what do you say?"

He jumped when, right behind him, a wolf whistle sounded and a cretinous voice cawed, *"I love yew!"*

There was of course a rational explanation for the mynah bird's presence on the bridge after dark. What with all the lights blazing for the first time since they sneaked out of Tarakan harbor, it must have found it hard to fall asleep. Even so, he took it as a personal affront. The hell with the nun. Let her haunt him till the cows came home and see where it got her.

That must be the problem with living in limbo—or wherever it was ghosts fooled around. It must give them the idea they could do anything: blow up Japanese MTB's, scare dogs, set mynah birds whistling at dead of night, turn Dyak tarts into Australian nurses; so why not make old Krasser do their bidding?

'Sister,' he thought, 'you have a surprise coming.'

PART FOUR

Hail and Farewell

1   The arrival of the *Henny* in Australia was sheer
fantasia. As she approached Fremantle, the port of Perth, a
small biplane circled overhead, pulling a streamer with some ad-
vertisement. It buzzed them, wiggled its wings in greeting; the
streamer said: WELCOME HENRY! GOOD SHOW! Everybody on
deck cheered; no one associated the message with themselves,
but the plane was a harbinger of freedom.

Only as the ship passed the outer buoy did it become clear
that the message had been intended for them: HENRY was a
misprint. Tugboats came out to meet them, pitching and rolling
under huge, swaying plumes squirted aloft by their water guns.
Foghorns boomed. Yachts decorated with pennants circled
around them. One, flying a Dutch flag as huge as a house, came
perilously close, wallowing in the wash of the tugboats, its deck
crammed with people. Voices were screaming the Dutch national anthem; the passengers of the *Henny* as well as those of
the yacht nearly threw themselves overboard waving, blowing

kisses, yelling. It was such a racket that Fifi peed on the bridge and the mynah bird, like a stuck gramophone record, went on wolf-whistling and cawing *"I love yew"* until Baradja, fearing it would suffer exhaustion, locked it in the toilet.

The first to board the ship was the harbor pilot, who shook hands with everybody, repeating, "Good show, folks, good show! Terrific! The whole town's come out to welcome you! Good show!" On the bridge the pilot said, pumping Krasser's hand after a startled encounter, "Captain, it's the greatest story to come out of the war so far! You managed to make us feel a lot better, all of us, not just the Dutch. The way you thumbed your nose at the Japs is what everyone has been wanting to do since Pearl Harbor! Boy, are you in for a reception!"

Krasser squinted up at him with a scowl of suspicion. "Reception?"

"You wait and see!" the pilot said. "All right, helmsman, pick up yonder red buoy."

The *Henny* moored alongside a quay massed with people; some were waving perilously from the tops of cranes. There was hooting of car horns and roaring of ships' sirens; on the quayside, schoolchildren waving little Dutch flags squealed *Waltzing Matilda* and the Dutch national anthem; a brass band, trombones flashing in the sun, kettle drums booming like cannon, blared *The Eton Boating Song*. And the moment the gangway was out, all hell broke loose.

Reporters and newsreel cameramen swarmed on deck. The Dutch consul and the mayor of Perth fought their way to the bridge to welcome the captain and inform him of the planned festivities. Krasser, with trembling Fifi in his arms, was told about a ticker-tape parade through town, the presentation of the key to the city on the steps of City Hall, a church service in the cathedral, a cocktail party at the Dutch Club, followed by a ball. Then tomorrow . . .

Krasser, flustered by newsreel cameramen yelling, "Give us

a smile, cap! How d'ye like Australia? How about a V sign?"
scurried into the chartroom, pursued by the lightning of flash-
bulbs. Baradja and Amu took refuge in the cabin, but were
traced by a female reporter. Mr. Faber the mortician, with com-
mendable presence of mind, safeguarded Dutch national honor
by stating that Baradja was the captain's wife and Amu his
daughter; nobody contradicted him.

To Herman, the reception was like an episode from *The Ara-
bian Nights*. It simply didn't seem real. The ecstatic cheers of the
Dutch colony, the throng of well-wishers, the radiant eyes, the
overwhelming goodwill, the embraces, the presumption that the
passengers had had anything to do with Krasser's feat of sea-
manship and daring—the whole thing seemed a comedy of
errors.

But gradually it dawned on him that the *Henny* was a symbol. Hers was the first victory for the humiliated white man in
Asia over the Japanese warlords who had beaten the Americans
and conquered three colonial empires in three months. Captain
Krasser, clutching his shivering dog, was like St. George: he had
tweaked the dragon's tail.

2

By the time the first photographs of Captain Benjamin Krasser, charming Mrs. Krasser, their beauteous daughter and Fifi, the ship's mascot, appeared in the papers the next morning something had been set in motion that could not be stopped until it had run its course. Captain Krasser was shepherded down the gangplank to the first of a row of open convertibles lined up on the quayside; the passengers piled into the rest.

To Herman, it was a surrealist experience. First the motorcade through the center of the city, where ticker tape and streamers of toilet paper came floating down from high office buildings and cheering throngs packed the sidewalk while mounted police kept them from mobbing the cars. Herman sat squeezed between Stotyn and Mr. Faber in the rumble seat of the last automobile in the procession. With the others, he waved at the crowd and the heads in the windows from which the paper came floating down, shouting, "Thank you! Thank you, Australia! Thank you, Perth!"

Mrs. de Winter, sitting beside the driver, waved graciously as if she were the Queen acknowledging the tribute of her adoring subjects. The whole thing was one huge carnival; it was also a bit of a mess. Hardly surprising, considering the reception must have been improvised in a matter of hours.

The church service in the cathedral was fairly ragged. Cheering throngs pressed at the doors; halfway through the sermon a booming voice yelled, "Get on with it, bishop!" The reception on the steps of City Hall consisted of rousing speeches and flashing bulbs and culminated in pint-size Captain Krasser being handed the key to the city, which he held awkwardly until Amu took it from him and put it in her purse. He held on to Fifi all the time as if for protection; the little dog, ears back, licking its nose, was photographed more often that morning than most heads of state in a month.

The culmination of the riotous day was a cocktail party, followed by banquet and ball, at the Dutch Club: a gloomy hall decked with flags, with a horseshoe of tables laid for supper on a dais at the far end, a thronelike armchair in its center. The passengers, Herman among them, were herded behind the tables; Captain Krasser was put on the throne like a child in a booster seat, flanked by his women, Fifi on his lap. He looked bewildered, and no wonder. They all were, with the exception of Mrs. de Winter, who installed herself next to the Dutch consul and acknowledged the ensuing parade of banners with a regal smile.

The banners, carried aloft by prominent members of the Dutch colony in Perth, showed the coats-of-arms of the eleven provinces of the Netherlands; each in turn was marched to the fore as the name of its province was bellowed by a master of ceremonies. It all seemed quaint and humorous to Herman, as one embroidered banner after another was dipped to honor the captain and marched off again. When the province of Friesland was called, Herman's heart skipped a beat: its standard bearer was Mrs. Bohm.

It took him a moment to recognize her, as she was wearing a large straw hat decorated with fruit and a blue ribbon tied in a bow under her chin. She looked calm, composed and radiant, exactly as she had up to the last minute during the destruction of Rauwatta. She was a vision of sanity despite her banner; he wanted to jump up, shout "Hey!" or "Josie!" but all he did was wave. She did not look at him; she dipped her banner in front of the captain, who sat clutching his dog like a lifebuoy; she obviously had not yet spotted Herman, but seeing her was so full of promise and generous sensuality, waiting only for him, that his eyes filled with tears as he grinned like an idiot, waving.

From that moment on he lost track of the proceedings. Speeches were made, food was served, wine poured, toasts proposed, a dance orchestra struck up *"Roll out the barrel,"* and the first couples made their way uncertainly to the floor. Herman, emboldened by hazardous helpings of Australian wine, strode to the table where Mrs. Bohm was sitting in a circle of beery men. "May I have this dance?"

The men scowled. Mrs. Bohm said, smiling under her hat, "Hello, Manny," put down her glass, rose and moved into his arms.

They went prancing away into the crowd to the tune of *The Beer Barrel Polka.* He gazed into her Delft-blue eyes, grinned inanely and said, "Well, here we go again. What on earth happened to you?"

Mrs. Bohm smiled. She looked more bucolic than ever with that hat, as if she had just got up from milking a cow. Then she said, "I'm with the consulate in Melbourne. I'm here to coordinate your reception. Nice to see you again, Manny-boy."

It seemed inconceivable that at one time he had reared at the name. It took all his self-control not to bawl on her shoulder.

She must have seen something in his eyes, for she tried to

kiss him, but the hat got in the way. The kiss, though aborted, was a confirmation of all she stood for: independence, reckless- ness and earthy warmth. He blurted out, "Can we go someplace after this? We have so much to talk about. . . . "

Her eyes searched his while her hands absent-mindedly ap- plauded after the Barrel had been Rolled Out. As the band struck up *Big Noise from Winnetka*, she said calmly, "I don't see why not," put an arm around his neck which startled him again by its weight, then took off with him as if she were heading for their tryst then and there. Bobbing among the dancers goose- stepping in post-prandial ebullience, she said, "A friend of mine has lent me her apartment. She's Hungarian and deals in an- tiques; she's on the road this week. Have they told you where you're staying?"

"No," he said, "I haven't been told anything. I'm just a log carried along by the current. Can you imagine how I felt, arriv- ing here? Tossed into a motorcade, covered with toilet paper thrown from the windows of skyscrapers—the whole thing's like a dream. Are you real?"

She grinned and hugged him briefly. It was exhilarating, but left a dull ache in his rib cage. "I'm so glad you made it," she said.

He grinned back. "So am I. Tell me, how did you get here? To Australia?"

She said, "Later," and dedicated herself to the dance.

It took a few more hours of dancing and, ultimately, a choked rendition of the national anthem before he found himself alone with Josie Bohm and her hat in a tiny automobile, whiz- zing through the deserted streets at midnight. They pulled up in front of a block of apartments; she yanked up the hand brake, put the gear shift in reverse, wormed herself out of the tiny vehi- cle and locked the door. Anyone planning to steal that car would have to carry it away under his arm. "This way," she said.

They entered through a side door to which she had the key,

marched down a dim corridor to a deserted lobby, where they took an elevator. He was rather drunk and full of adolescent anticipation; at the same time he had an odd feeling of farewell, as if his image of Josie Bohm, precious and infinitely tender, cherished since the mountains, was about to change.

The door when opened let out a genteel scent of beeswax and snuffed candles. She switched on a hall light and strode down a passage hung with Pre-Raphaelite paintings like a gallery. A door at the far end revealed a bedroom full of draped curtains with tassels and Biedermeier furniture, dominated by a huge rococo four-poster bed. She lit candles on the mantel and the bedside table, turned off the lights and said, "Well now— where were we?"

Without waiting for his reply, she took him in her arms and kissed his lips. It was exciting, yet he remained curiously detached. He could not forget the hat, the scent of beeswax, the ancestral portraits gazing down upon them from the walls with faint distaste. She kissed him long and arduously; he managed a response that was not without passion; then she held him at arms' length and said with a satisfied sigh, "Ah! I needed that!" She must have read his detachment in his eyes, for she added, "Didn't you?"

"I've thought so much about you," he said evasively. "I was lost in the mountains, hallucinating, for God knows how long. Thanks to your alpenstock and your brochure, I made it. I was the only one."

Her eyes searched his. "You mean: all the men . . . ?"

"Intercepted by a Japanese patrol as we were waiting to cross the Rokul road. I think the guide may have escaped, but no one else."

"Killed? All of them?"

"Maybe there were prisoners. I didn't count the bodies. I was out of range and lay behind a boulder all day; by the time I came out the vultures had worked them over."

"Sam Hendriks too?" she asked, her eyes suddenly full of grief.

So Sam Hendriks and she had been lovers. He suppressed the puerile jealousy and said, "I didn't see him; at least, I don't think I did. It was hard to say who was who; I only recognized Palstra and Imhof. After that, I'd had enough."

"Poor sweetie," she said, hugging him. "What a terrible experience. No wonder you look washed out."

He had not been aware that he did.

"All right," she said briskly, shaking the specter of death, "once more into the fray." She started to unbutton her dress with calm competence, like a Channel swimmer preparing for her stint. Seeing him standing there indecisively, she urged, "Come on!" When she stood naked, after what seemed only a matter of seconds, she still had her hat on.

"Are you going to stay fully dressed?" she asked.

"You—er—you know you're still wearing your hat?"

She hesitated, then she undid the bow, took it off and tossed it aside. When she faced him again she smiled unsurely and he realized that the purpose of the ribbon had been to hold up a double chin; she had indeed put on weight. He felt embarrassed for her, so he hastily undressed, as if the sight of her without hat had aroused his passion. Rubens would have thrown himself on her with the goat cry of creativity; all *he* wanted was to hide under the blankets.

She drew back the bedspread, opened the covers, fluffed the pillows, climbed in with a display of pendulous breasts and massive buttocks, lay back and patted the empty space beside her. Feeling thin and slight, he joined her.

"Ah!" she said, bent over him, kissed him and swept him up in such a surge of passion that after a stunned moment he let himself be towed under. He had often imagined what it would be like to make love to Josie Bohm; reality disposed of those bloodless fantasies in seconds. It was not he who made love to her but the other way around. A daughter of Neptune, frolicking in the waves, not with her lover, let alone her master, but with a plaything, a rubber duck, a dolphin's ball. Heavings, tossings, grunts, trumpetings; a battle of gods, he told himself frantically while being caught in hammerlocks and crushed in massive embraces. It was exciting, yet there was his alter ego, the detached observer, who looked at the scene as Rubens would have done: *Nymph and Satyr,* thin, hairy limbs frantically protruding from an avalanche of luminous flesh in a swaying four-poster, its curtains swinging, frightened cherubs clutching its posts. Cherubs . . . suddenly, with ghoulish clarity, there was Mr. Imhof's dimpled back, his eyeless body crumpled at the foot of the boulder.

Then Josie Bohm, in the throes of an awe-inspiring climax, heaved their combined weight up in the air, fell back, and with a tremendous splintering sound the four-poster collapsed on top of them as they crashed through the bed.

Both of them lay still for a few moments; then she said, "Hell's bells!" and started to dig herself out of the tangle of pillars, canopy, pillows, tasseled curtains and quilt. When they finally emerged, they contemplated the wreckage, side by side. She said, "God! Esther is going to be furious! Let's see if we can put the damn thing back together for now. Are you good with your hands?"

"Fair to middling."

"All right, let's have a go."

Together they tried to resurrect the four-poster leveled by love. He wasn't much use, but she turned out to be very good with her hands. She started by putting the pillars back up, removing the curtains and the bedding; then she stepped inside the frame and tried to put the bottom planks back in place, all this while stark naked. It took nearly an hour; in the end the rococo four-poster once more dominated the room, its phony massiveness restored, but in such precarious balance that a passing truck might bring the whole structure crashing down again.

"Well," she said, surveying the result of her labor with satisfaction. "That looks pretty good, doesn't it?"

"Yes . . ."

She took him in her arms and said, her blue eyes very close, her breath warm on his mouth, "Did I leave you high and dry, Manny-boy? If not, I may have left it rather late."

"Don't worry," he said. "It hit me earlier."

Her eyes searched his as she sensed his detachment, which had now won the day. Then she kissed him. "Let's go and find another bed," she said. "I know there is one."

He did not really want to be taken in a full nelson again and tossed aloft, but he followed her obediently. She opened a few doors, said, "Here it is," and threw herself onto a queen-size double bed. "This one's all right. Let's give it a whirl."

He lay down beside her. She put out an arm for his head to rest on. "Tell me," she said.

"Tell you what?"

"What happened to you after we said goodbye at the airport."

"I told you: we got lost in the mountains. The others were shot; I managed to reach the mouth of the river, where the *Henny* picked me up."

"You were lucky, lover. Like a drunk crossing the road."

"What happened to you after you took off in that plane?"

"Nothing much," she said, as casually as he. "I got to Batavia, joined the Ministry of Information. When Java fell I was evacuated to Australia with the rest of the staff. So, here I am. Here *we* are."

"Yes."

"Gosh, I'm tired." She yawned, slumped; almost at once her breathing slowed and her massive limbs twitched in the onset of sleep.

He lay still, listening to her breathing. Rauwatta. The Hôtel des Indes. Their first kiss, interrupted by the manager. "War!

War!" It seemed a lifetime ago. He had little in common these days with the Herman Winsum who had sat at the table in the conference room, shuffling candids of the Rauwatta *beau monde*. As for her, she seemed exactly the same, only heavier and maybe more promiscuous. He had no illusion about her having pined for him all these months, despite her passionate assurances to that effect at the height of her ecstasy. She had enjoyed him as she would a generous helping of Black Forest cake; now, replete and sated, she was sleeping it off.

Gazing at the ceiling, her naked amplitude warm beside him, he asked himself why he had been spared. 'Like a drunk crossing the road.' Was that really all there was to it? She started to snore.

Suddenly, tears ran down his cheeks. He turned on his side, threw a leg across her sturdy thighs, an arm across her stomach, and tried to sleep. She grunted, turned around with a mighty heave, and the Delft-blue eyes, larger than life, opened right in front of his. She kissed him. "What are you planning to do here in Australia, Manny-boy?"

"No idea. I haven't quite arrived yet."

"Well, leave it to me. I'll find you a nice job somewhere, in Melbourne. I have plenty of contacts."

"I'll bet you do." She must have a whale of a time here in Australia, frolicking in the pastures of peace. "I don't think—" he started, but she cut him short.

"You needn't think. I'll fix it. I know just who to tackle on this."

Somehow, he was failing her; not physically but creatively. Ah, for Rubens' zest and prodigious vitality! He should have ripped one of the brocade curtains off the four-poster, thrown it around her creamy shoulders, put her on the bed leaning on one elbow with that sly sidelong glance of sensuous anticipation, and called it *Potiphar's Wife Awakening*.

But, alas, he was no Rubens. He just wrote about him.

3 Krasser was awakened from a dream in his hotel by the sound of someone being sick in the bathroom. Both girls were there, fast asleep, one on each side of him. It must be Fifi.

Sure enough, after a short silence she appeared in the doorway crestfallen, ears back, licking her nose. Krasser closed his eyes and tried to pick up the dream: something about birds. A great space; the gackering of seagulls; a ship's wake.

But he could not recapture that world of freedom and happiness now he had wakened in the reality of snoring tarts and a dog throwing up in the bathroom. Suddenly, he was overcome by a sense of loss, loneliness, grief—a hangover of the soul. There was his ship, alone at the quayside, with Kwan Chan in command. He'd better get back on board; even with the Australian Navy lined up outside, the bastard was capable of sneaking out unseen. He had had excellent training.

Krasser lay gazing at the ceiling, a girl's head on each shoulder, Fifi peering onto the bed between his feet. What would become of him? What would become of his ship? Despite the brass band, the parade, the blizzard of paper, the cheering crowds, the key to the city, he felt trapped. For thirty years he had been master of his own fate; now he was a sitting duck for whichever jackass was in charge of Dutch shipping. A three-star general with a bald head and a bank of medals on his chest had talked down to him during the festivities last night. "Captain, you and I must have a serious talk."

"About what?"

The answer, with a smile of gleaming dentures, had been, "Your future."

Amu stirred and turned over. Fifi kept her baleful stare fixed on him level with the blankets, a silent plea to join them. That was all he needed: a dog that had just been sick. He had to get out of here.

He slid out of bed without waking the girls, which wasn't difficult; once they slept you could walk over them and they would go on snoring; they slept through gales, thunderstorms, naval battles and only awoke when they smelled food.

He started to dress, observed by Fifi. He would have liked to kick her out, for it bothered him to dress in front of a dog that unblinkingly followed all his movements. Tucking her under his arm when he was done, he waddled to the door. On the floor lay a sheet of paper covered with bossy handwriting: *As there is some rivalry between the Mothers' Union and the Women's Institute, I suggest your ladies accept the Union's invitation for luncheon and participate in this evening's whist drive organized by the Institute. I'll meet them at eleven o'clock in the lobby. Josephine Bohm, Government Information Service.* He dropped it back on the floor and sneaked out.

He had no idea what the time was; it must still be early. It might be difficult to find a taxi at this hour to take him to the harbor. When he stepped out into the street in the young sunlight, Fifi under his arm, a chauffeur in Army uniform jumped from a waiting limousine, opened the door for him and said, "Good morning, captain."

"Who the hell are you?"

"General Kalman's driver, sir. The general is expecting you."

"Where?"

"In his office, sir."

Krasser considered ignoring the invitation, but it might be prudent to stay on the right side of the general. So he got in and climbed onto the luxurious seat, Fifi on his lap. The car drove fast, whispering through empty streets toward the east end of town, then down a wide boulevard skirting the Swan River until it arrived at a gate in a wall which opened at its approach and closed after it had passed inside. They drove up to a large house, where the general with the bald head welcomed him on the steps, hand outstretched; the guard at the gate must have alerted him. "Captain Krasser! A rare pleasure!"

"All right if I bring my dog?"

"Of course! Delighted!" The general preceded him down a corridor and opened the door to an office. "Do sit down. Make yourself comfortable."

Krasser sat down opposite a desk, Fifi on his lap. She started to tremble. He hoped the general would not throw his rank about, or she might pee.

The general sat down behind the desk, gave him a smile of Japanese teeth and said, "That was quite a reception they gave you!"

Krasser grunted.

"I must say, well deserved. The feat you performed was truly epochal."

"Excuse me?"

"You are that precious phenomenon in times of mortal national danger: a true hero."

Fifi's trembling increased.

"Now—after a decent interval of recuperation—we'd like to

177

profit further from your genius," the general continued. "By 'we' I mean the Fatherland."

Krasser stroked Fifi's head.

"What interests us is your genius for camouflage. To sail down the coasts of Borneo, Billiton and Sumatra without being spotted is a rare gift, captain. Most useful to the cause."

Fifi heaved. Krasser wondered whether to let her be sick on the general's carpet or to ask for the bathroom. He could lock her in there while they went on discussing his genius for camouflage.

"Let me explain, captain." The general reclined so far in his chair that he appeared to fall backward; then he lifted his feet onto the desk. The soles of his shoes were new. That seemed reassuring; maybe he wasn't as experienced at his job as he pretended to be.

"What I'm about to tell you is Top Secret, captain. You must give me your word of honor that you won't breathe one syllable of it to others, whoever they may be."

Krasser promised.

"The entire territory of the Dutch East Indies is now in Japanese hands. We cannot sit back and wait for others to reclaim it for us. We do not at present have the power to stage a full-fledged invasion, but we can at least keep the Jap on his toes, pin down a few garrisons he might otherwise send to theaters of war where they might tip the balance. Briefly, we are preparing commando raids on New Guinea. They'll be hazardous. The men we parachute into the jungle will have to fend for themselves. They'll have to live off the land, blend into the local population. The Papuans are violently anti-Japanese, so we may count on their cooperation. But the amount of ammunition our men can carry when they're dropped is limited. This is where you come in."

Fifi gave a violent heave. The general looked concerned. "Is your dog all right?"

"For the moment," Krasser said.

"H'm. Well—given your ability to disappear into the wood-work with your vessel, we want you to supply our commandos after they're dropped. We'll decide on an assembly point some-where along the coast, a cove or inlet. You sneak in there, un-load your cargo and return to base until the next sortie." The general flashed his man-made grin. "It may sound simple," he said, "but we wouldn't ask anybody else to even try. You are the only man for the job."

"Thank you," Krasser said.

"I realize you'll want to think this over," the general con-tinued, picking up a signal. "Give it some thought, then let me hear from you. We cannot force you to accept this mission, but you no doubt know what the score is." He rose; another grin, a handshake, abortive because it made Fifi growl. Then he said, "Where do you want my chauffeur to drop you, captain? Your hotel?"

"I want to go back on board."

"Very well. When may I have the pleasure of seeing you again?" He did not wait for an answer. "Shall we say day after tomorrow, fifteen hundred hours?"

Krasser gave him a meaningless look and said nothing.

The general opened the door. "See you then, captain."

The driver was sitting on a chair in the corridor and leaped to his feet as the captain appeared.

"Corporal!" the general barked. "Take the captain to his ship! Know where that is?"

"Yes, sir."

It was a long, silent drive back to town and out the other side, then all the way to Fremantle Harbor. The driver tried to make conversation, but was silenced by the lack of response. Finally they pulled up at the gangway, among the rails and the cranes. The driver opened the door. "I'll wait, sir."

"No need to," Krasser said. "I'll make my own way back."

The driver saluted, got back into his car, but stayed where he was.

The first to welcome the captain was the mynah bird. Fifi yapped and wagged her tail; Krasser realized it wasn't he who was being welcomed but the dog. He let Fifi go the moment they reached the deck, and she ran off, chasing the bird. Kwan Chan appeared, smiling, and wanted to start a conversation, but was discouraged.

Alone in his chartroom, surrounded by his familiar reality, Krasser stared down at the chart of the Pacific and shook his head. He was not about to let the general with the porcelain teeth use his ship for murder. Dropping commandos in occupied New Guinea was murder. Not one of those kids would come back alive. After three hundred years of Dutch rule, the Papuans, like the Dyaks, must be in a frenzy of freedom and independence; no white man dropping from the sky in camouflage suit and helmet covered with twigs would have a ghost of a chance. If Twinkleteeth wanted somebody dropped in the jungle of New Guinea to show the flag, let him drop himself. The *Henny* was not going to cooperate, never mind what 'the score' was.

He was still looking at the chart when Fifi arrived to spy out the land, her eyes level with the threshold.

"All right, slut," he said, "come in."

She came in and was given the atheist's cookie.

4

That night there was another celebration, the second that day: a whist drive organized by the Women's Institute in which all passengers of the *Henny* including Herman were invited to take part. The first event of the day had been a luncheon given by the Mothers' Union, for which Mrs. Krasser and her beauteous daughter had been urged to provide an Indonesian dish. The two ladies had obliged; after the first few bites some of the assembled mothers had gasped, hoarsely asking for water. Asked what the incendiary ingredient was, Mrs. Krasser had answered proudly, *"Sambal deng-deng."*

Captain Krasser, dragged to the whist drive virtually in chains, was presented with a shearling coat. Josie Bohm joined Herman while the presentation was in progress and whispered, "I fixed it." When he asked, "Fixed what?" she put her finger to his lips and said, "Hush! Later!" Finally, after the anthems had been sung and the crowd was dispersing, she put her arm through his and said, "Come, *snoepje.*"

"Where are we going?"

"Esther's flat. She's gone all week."

They drove at breakneck speed back to the apartment building and Esther's flat; the moment they stepped inside, she put her arms around him and kissed him with abandon while closing the door with her foot. Then she virtually dragged him to the living room, where she tipped him onto the sofa, lowered herself on top of him and breathed in his hair, "I have just the job for you. A sinecure, well paid, not far from Melbourne—a peach."

"What is it?" he asked in a strangled voice.

"Editor of a Dutch-language weekly for a rural community of immigrants. Just being settled, in the outback. Sheep farmers, mostly. The job has a house and an *Abo* housekeeper thrown in. Good salary. And you can handle it with one hand tied behind your back. Lots of free time, Manny-boy. Lots of business trips to Melbourne for interviews, conventions—you name it. I'll keep you posted."

"Where—er—is it an existing paper?"

"Oh yes. But just. Guy who tried to make a go of it packed up and left for a government job. But he was an incompetent slob. You'll make that little darling sing. It has a cute name, too. The *Hopalong Clarion*."

"You're kidding."

"Why? Don't you think it's cute? Hopalong is the name of the town. Well—'town,' it's barely off the ground, and you're going to be in on the building of it. Exciting, isn't it?"

He didn't know whether to laugh or cry, and ended by doing both. She understood; it was "the reaction." She was overwhelming in her affection; he had occasionally heard rumors about men being raped and never understood how that was technically possible; now he discovered what it meant.

She subjected another of her Hungarian friend's pieces of antique furniture to the crash test; he ended up cradled in her arms on the now lopsided sofa, his back and buttocks getting cold as they protruded over the edge. She heaved a voluptuous

182

sigh, opened her eyes close to his, kissed his nose and said, "How about saying 'thank you'?"

For a moment he thought that she expected gratitude for the workout, then he realized she was referring to the weekly with the hilarious name. "Where exactly is it?" he asked.

"Three hundred miles from Mel. Exactly what I wanted you to have: a sinecure. Lots of sleep, no social demands . . . " She grinned and kissed his nose again. "You need R-and-R. That's what you need."

"But aren't I supposed to enlist? Report for military service?"

"No," she replied, yawning. "I fixed it with old what's-his-name. The job is considered to be in the national interest."

"Who's old what's-his-name?"

She rolled onto her side, slapped his bottom and said, "Let's eat."

She climbed over him and set out toward the kitchenette. There she put on an apron and began to clatter and bang with pots and pans, her nakedness only symbolically covered with the little apron. For some reason, seeing her like that aroused him: stark naked, vigorously scouring a frying pan, a bawdy picture of domesticity, of uncomplicated, earthy emotions directly expressed. Whatever his rank and serial number in her army of lovers might be, while they were together she gave him all she had. Her jolly randiness temporarily made him forget the emptiness of his lonely condition.

She did everything with zest: cook, slice bread, slam ice trays on the counter; she opened a bottle of wine, holding it between her thighs as she yanked out the cork. "Sorry," she said, "Esther has no hard liquor, only vino and liqueurs. So let's try this." She filled two tumblers to the brim. "Here's to Hopalong." She took a deep draft, smacked her lips, then took a second one.

He joined her behind the counter, put his arms around her and made overtures, but she slapped his hand and said, "Time and place for everything! Let's have something to eat first."

She laid the table, lit candles, put him in his chair and virtually tied his napkin around his neck; the only thing lacking was a booster seat. The meal turned out to be excellent, and the wine, certainly in the quantities she made him indulge in, filled him with a glow of hedonism. Over coffee, fingering a brandy glass of Austrian liqueur with the odd name of *Klimaxfahrt*, gazing at the candle flame in the green liquid as he slowly turned his glass around, he realized that he was falling in love. Then he heard her say, "Don't be gloomy, honey. Give yourself time."

"What?"

She was sitting opposite, her blue eyes observing him; in his hazy state of inebriation it looked as if her nipples were observing him too. *Four-eyed Minotaur, brooding in his cave.* "What do you mean?"

"I know it's hard to forget," she said, sipping her drink. "I myself wake up at night occasionally in a sweat, dreaming about them. I find that all you can do is work at forgetting them. They have no business in your life; they're dead. As the Frogs say: '*Arrière, cadavres.*'"

"Who are you talking about?"

She shrugged, a supple movement of coordinated orbs and ovals in the candlelight. "Corpses. Dear corpses. I've seen enough of them to last me a lifetime. The hell with them. Life is for the living. Let the dead bury the dead."

For a moment it seemed as if she were offering him as escape from despair; then he recognized the difference between them. She might have seen scenes as gruesome as he had, but she had not been responsible for them. He was about to blurt out the truth, tell her about the column that had broken behind his back, how all the men of Rauwatta would have crossed the road safely if only he'd had the guts or the sense to call 'Stop!' But he suppressed the impulse. She would try to impose on him her own approach, a projection of her own abundant vitality, which, alas, he did not share. Compared to her, he was a prissy intellectual without guts or gumption, forced to arrive at all crucial decisions in his life cerebrally because his physical current was too low to produce an impulse strong enough to change the course of his destiny.

"Come to bed," she said, bunching up her napkin and tossing it on the table. "Let's get rid of the glooms."

He rose; it was his last voluntary act for the rest of the evening. She took him back to the bedroom with the queen-size bed, still unmade after last night's match, and made love to him with such abandon that his body responded. But his emotions were left cold, for she made love with the same voracious single-mindedness with which she had demolished the food and knocked back the wine; he was part of the menu. She wallowed, panting, up the spiral of ecstasy with gale-force sighs reeking of *Klimaxfahrt;* she heaved him around on the twanging bed like a Great Dane romping with a Dachshund. His body joined her rafter-rattling catharsis, but it was as if his soul looked down ruefully, somewhere underneath the ceiling, at the contortions of their frenzied flesh.

Finally, their passion spent, they lay side by side among the tousled bedclothes damp with sweat. Suddenly a wish struck him, with the randomness of a stone hurled from space: if only he could *do* something—anything—to redeem his betrayal of the forty-seven who had died because of him!

Again, a cerebral wish, the lifeless outcome of reasoning, not an overpowering impulse from the vital core of his being. He wanted to be forgiven, not to atone.

But who was there to forgive him, other than the forty-seven men from Rauwatta? And, judged by the tenacity with which they haunted him, they were not about to. He could not even forgive himself. There would have to be an atonement.

"What are you thinking about, Manny?"

For a moment, he was tempted to tell her; then he realized she would take issue with him, furiously.

"What is an *Abo* housekeeper?" he asked.

"A native. Like *babu.* It's short for Aborigine. They're very ugly. But I'll check on her all the same."

The urge to confess had passed. "You do that," he said.

185

5

Krasser, slumped in the swivel chair in his chart-room with his feet sticking out, knocked back his fourth glass of gin even though it was only nine o'clock in the morning. He was furious.

When he had arrived by taxi on the quayside an hour earlier and climbed the gangway he had found the ship deserted again, not a single bloody soul. The men must have been boozing and whoring all night and were now getting over their hangover somewhere ashore. The only one around was some native *klootzak* appointed watchman by Kwan Chan before he sneaked off himself. The *klootzak* was asleep in the galley when Krasser arrived; some watchman! The mynah bird did a better job.

He had the ship all to himself; the girls were off with the fatso from the consulate. None of the passengers had bothered to come back either—here he was, alone with Fifi, the bird and Rip Van Winkle in the galley. Enough to drive a man to drink.

Krasser's mood became worse as he brooded about the gen-

186

eral with the Japanese teeth who wanted to feed the Papuans cannon fodder from the air. Never in a thousand years. But what was the alternative? He knew what 'the score' was.

While he stood, for the umpteenth time, on his stool bent over the chart of the Pacific wondering where the hell to go, a car stopped on the quayside and its doors slammed. He went out on the bridge and climbed onto the platform to see who it was. A small red automobile, no more than a motorized suppository, was parked at the bottom of the gangway; some joker was coming up the gangway, he could not make out who; all he could see was the top of the man's head. "Hey!" he called.

The visitor looked up. It was the young journalist he had picked up in the mouth of the Kali Woga. He neither liked nor disliked the guy, easily the most forgettable among his passengers, but he felt so gloomy that he called, "Come up to the bridge. Have a snort!"

When the young man appeared on the bridge he was handed a glass, ready filled. "Come in," Krasser said. "Let's sit here, in the messroom."

After he had installed himself on the leatherette seat and the young man on the chair opposite, Krasser raised his glass. "Well, here's to our lost freedom."

The young man gave him a queer look. "I'll drink to that. What made you say it?"

Krasser normally resented having what he said picked over, but the youth was all there was to play with, so he replied grudgingly, "I mean our days of independence are over. We're back in civilization now: on with the chains, knuckle your forehead and curtsy. Know what they had the gall to ask me?"

He must be drunk, for there he went: telling the wishy-washy youth across the table about the general's murderous plan. He was irritated, not for betraying the general's trust—that was the general's business—but for blabbing like a woman across a back fence.

Not all that much could be said about the general's plan, however, other than that it was murder. "And I'll be triple damned if I let myself and my ship be used for that. So: here's to freedom, boy. Let's you and me get the hell back to the sea and the jungle." Quite a little speech. Disgusted, he poured himself the sixth, or seventh; he had lost count.

Then the young man on the other side of the table asked, "Do we have a choice, captain? Do we ever really have a choice?"

"You bet your *piemel* we have," Krasser replied firmly; he was not about to carry his drunken confession to the point where he admitted he hadn't.

"It never occurred to me you felt so strongly about these things," the youth said after a silence which had gone unnoticed, as Krasser had forgotten his presence. The words 'the sea and the jungle' had evoked with harrowing nostalgia a vision of peace, solitude, sovereignty: alone with his ship, his dog and his women on the shifting shades of blue and green of the Pond of the Dead, with the whirl of birdsound ashore, the sweet, nutty smell of the marshes. "What was that you said?"

"It seems unlike you to worry about someone's lack of respect for individual life."

It was too deep for Krasser, after six snorts. This conversation wasn't going anywhere; for a few moments it had relieved his gloom, now it turned into a bore. But the loneliness was like physical pain; he simply could not bear being left in this empty messroom, or hanging around in the chartroom waiting for something to happen, some sign of promise or hope. "You believe in ghosts?" he asked abruptly.

The young man pursed his lips, composing a polite answer. To forestall him, Krasser continued, "I don't either, but there have been—well—happenings. You know about the broken cable of number-one winch?" The youth shook his head and started to say something; Krasser plowed it under. Boy, that rotgut was wicked stuff. But what harm could it do to tell the story of the winch? Of Fifi growling as she followed the progress of an invisible presence on the bridge? Of the mynah bird drawing attention to the squeal of the bearing that had run dry? Of Baradja imagining she heard him call for 'drinkies'? He poured himself another drinkie and sallied into his repertoire of ghost stories about the nun.

He sensed that the youth was responding. Not to the stories maybe, but to the memory of the shared adventure, the call of the sea. Boy, he was drunk. "Well," he said, "I think I'll have a snooze. I've had a busy night. Anything else I can do for you?" He needed to stretch out on the seat; the messroom was now rising and falling around him.

"I don't think it was her ghost, captain."

"Huh?"

"It's not her ghost we can't forget. It's her spirit."

Krasser did not comment; he lay down, closed his eyes and fell asleep.

6

Krasser did not know how long he had lain there, asleep on the sweat-slick seat in the messroom, when he was awakened by a woman's voice calling, "Captain! Hey, captain!"

It was the fatso with the hat full of fruit, the organizer of the folderol.

"Wakey-wakey!" she said breezily, stepping inside. "Come on, man! You're needed!"

"What for?"

"Special invitation from His Excellency the Governor General: supper tomorrow in the palace in Canberra for yourself, the Netherlands Ambassador and your two ladies. We leave by plane in about three hours. Show me what you have in the way of uniforms. Was the one you were wearing last night your best?"

"Now, look here . . . "

"That was okay for Perth, but for the Governor General you need something that doesn't make you look as if you'd come to read the gas meter. Hop to it, my friend! I've already started fitting out your two ladies, now it's your turn. Up! Up!" She held out her hand to pull him off the seat.

The last thing he wanted was to go to somebody's palace for a gala dinner and make a spectacle of himself, but this was one powerful lady and he was too hung over to put up a fight.

On the quayside the same tiny red automobile the journalist had arrived in stood waiting; it was a miracle the woman could squeeze herself into it, let alone the two of them. The damn thing took off like a kangaroo before his door was closed; the woman drove like a demon unleashed. She had him scared out of his wits by the time she skidded to a stop outside a department store.

"Out! I'll park the car, you go up to Men's Formal Clothing, second floor to the right, and ask for uniforms. I'll join you as soon as I've made sure your ladies are where they should be."

He watched her whizz off in the tiny machine, hating her with the bilious hatred of the helpless. Then he waddled inside and headed for the men's department.

He was being decked out in a uniform with a cap like a heliport and accordion trousers about which the salesman said, saccharinely, that they needed 'a slight adjustment' when the woman turned up, flustered. "Why didn't you tell me you've got kids?"

He gaped at her.

"What's this about a little boy with one leg?"

"A what?"

"Your wife is creating an uproar downstairs in the kids' department, buying a football boot for a ten-year-old. She says she'll only pay for one because that's all he needs."

He said, "You're crazy, lady."

She took it in her stride. "Well, somebody is! I can't reason with the woman, so you go down and tell her to cut it out. She can't break up a pair of shoes; see if you can get that through her thick skull. No offense intended. This way." Silencing the salesman with a look, she strode off and, forgetting about his clown's outfit, he waddled after her. The whole thing had a hallucinatory quality, like the beginning of delirium tremens. In the boys' department, between racks of children's shoes, he found Baradja clutching one boot and glowering at a suave gentleman obviously brought in to appease her.

"What the hell's going on here?" Krasser asked. "What do you want that for?"

"For the little boy," she said, in a tone that promised no compromise. She was a docile soul, but, as with a mule, there came a moment when she became immobile and took root.

There were nosy people around, mouths open, looking him up and down; he caught a glimpse of himself in a mirror at the far end of the aisle and grabbed her by the arm. "Come with me!" To the fat woman he said, "Pay for the shoes, I'll pay you back. I'll talk to her."

Baradja allowed herself to be towed into a corner, clutching her boot. There she looked down on him defiantly with the expression women have when something in their moon-ruled minds gets jammed. No use arguing with her under the circumstances; so all he asked was, "What boy are you talking about?"

"The retarded one the nun taught how to lace a shoe. He lost it in the forest, so I bought him a new one."

He gazed up at her with a sense of awe. There she stood, flat-nosed, slit-eyed, stupid, degraded, yet suddenly she gave him a feeling he wouldn't have associated with her in a thousand years: respect. "You don't think we're going *back*, do you?"

Baradja looked at him with those determined eyes and said, "Of course we are!"

"Why?"

"Because you promised." From the way she said it, it was obvious she had never doubted for a second that he would.

He heard the bossy woman behind him ask something, but he wasn't listening. He stared at Baradja for a moment, then he said, "Let me get dressed," and turned away.

As they walked back to the men's department, the woman carried on about "cummerbunds," but he still wasn't listening.

It had never occurred to him that there was someone in the world who took him to be a man of honor.

7   When Herman was ushered into the presence of Albert Haversma, head of the Netherlands Government Information Service, he was surprised. He did not know what he had expected, but not the portly old man who rose behind his desk, crying, "Winsum! Splendid! I'm so glad to see you! Sit down! Please!" As Herman had never set eyes on the man, he wondered to what he owed this enthusiasm.

Haversma leaned forward and looked at him with paternal fondness. There was something out of kilter in the image he presented; Herman could not put his finger on it. "Cigar?" Haversma proffered a box. "No? Cigarette?" Another box.

"No, thank you," Herman said, "I don't smoke."

"You don't mind if I light up, do you?" Haversma struck a match, lit a cigar, waved out the flame, blew the first smoke and looked at his visitor with avuncular affection. "I know all about you, Winsum. Mrs. Bohm told me. Of course I'm delighted you're prepared to go to Hopalong. Gracious of you to and square it with me. Like yourself, I'm sensitive to the few civilized niceties left to us."

Herman cleared his throat, then said, "I'm here to enlist."

"Enlist?" The smile hung on, but now it became obvious what had been out of kilter: the eyes. They did not share in the warmth the old man exuded, they were weary and without illusions, as if they had seen it all.

"I've come for accreditation as a war correspondent. I'd like to be assigned to the commandos who are about to be dropped in New Guinea."

Haversma froze. "Who told you that?"

"Something I picked up."

"Picked up where?"

"I'm not at liberty to say. I have to protect my source."

Haversma swiveled his chair and looked out the window. Woolly little clouds, like sheep, drifted peaceably into the empty continent beyond. "I'm afraid I'll have to report this to General Kalman," he said finally.

"As you wish."

The chair swiveled back. "Can you give me an idea why you want that particular assignment? Let me add: in the unlikely case such an operation were contemplated at some time in the future, it certainly would not include war correspondents."

"As far as my involvement is concerned, I'd consider that a wrong decision."

"Why, may I ask?"

"Their chances of survival are slender, to say the least. If any group of men needs the presence of someone who's been through this before, it will be they."

The weary eyes contemplated him. "And where do you come in?"

"I escaped from the town of Rauwatta with forty-seven other men. I know first hand what it means to be lost in the jungle, without hope. I was the only survivor."

The old man sucked at his cigar, blew a ring at the ceiling which he followed with his eyes. Finally he asked, "You talked this over with Mrs. Bohm?"

194

Herman stiffened. "Why would I do that?"

Haversma put down his cigar. "Mrs. Bohm is a sensible woman. She seems to have taken a liking to you. I suggest you talk it over with her before I submit your request to the military."

"Could you tell me your rationale for that?"

The weary eyes gazed at him without illusions. "It's too soon after your recent experience for you to come to such a drastic decision, Winsum. Even supposing your request were to be considered, you owe it to yourself and to the men involved to recover from your emotional trauma first."

Herman rose. "I'll keep that phrase in mind, Mr. Haversma, for future use by war-weary correspondents."

But the old man was impervious to irony. The smile came back, so did the avuncular jollity. "You take care now, Winsum. Give yourself time to recuperate. Talk to Mrs. Bohm, she's a sensible woman. And don't go around spreading rumors about commando raids on New Guinea; that kind of loose talk could get a lot of people into trouble—including yourself, should the military grant your request." Haversma reached out; they shook hands. "Come and see me again in a month's time. Good luck—and enjoy life for a change."

On his way out Herman was overcome by a sense of desolation. During the few hours that he had been roaming the streets of Perth and wandering along the embankment of the river, looking at the yachts, it had not occurred to him that he might be turned down, let alone through the machinations of Josie Bohm, *éminence grise* of the Information Service.

Forlorn, he crossed the lobby to the exit; just then Josie came out of the elevator, swinging an attaché case. Obviously Haversma had done some telephoning, for she faced him like a cop and said, "You're out of your goddam mind!"

"Perth, home of the best-kept secrets," he joked lamely.

"Secrets, hell!" She grabbed his arm as if she were placing him under arrest. "You're sick! Let's go home."

Too tired to protest, he let himself be taken to the miniature car she called Little Root-toot and was driven off, prisoner of love.

8 "All right," she said, "let's hear it. I'm all ears."
She wasn't. She was all bosom and belly and opulent thighs and a navel straight from the Song of Solomon, now tasting salty. "Don't do that," she said. "It tickles."

He looked up and gazed at her Dutch eyes across the plain of Galilee, between the distant hills of Lebanon.

"Feel better now?" she asked.

"Hoary old joke," he said, kissing the downy rim of her belly button. *Thy navel is like a round goblet which wanteth not liquor; thy belly like a heap of wheat set about with lilies.*

"Can you talk about it now?"

"About what?"

"What you discussed with my friend."

"H'm," he said, kissing.

"All right, then! Talk!"

The sky of her eyes was clear and blue; something in its

196

tranquillity seduced him. But he did not want to be seduced. "First, I'll have a pee," he said.

He got up and padded to the john behind the seventeenth-century wet bar. There were funny-ha-ha pictures on the wall: a little boy peeing against a tree with a little girl watching and thinking: *'Oh, how practical!'* A color print of a collection of birds' eggs from some manual: *Eggs of Hungarian Birds.* An embroidered sampler with, in Gothic letters: *Some flow'rets of Eden ye still inherit, but the trail of the Serpent is over them all.* The words seemed oddly appropriate: the noble impulse for self-sacrifice run to seed, the flow'ret of atonement soiled by the Serpent's trail. What was the Serpent? Stupidity? Cowardice? Guilt? He flushed the toilet, washed his hands and went back to the bedroom.

She was still lying on her back on the queen-size bed, sleek and ample, her hands under her head. As he entered she turned her head; the blue eyes contemplated him with a languorous gaze.

"*Tant pis, tant mieux:* Auntie left the room, Auntie felt better," he joked.

She didn't laugh, maybe she knew the joke. She should, at her age. What was her age, anyway? Difficult to guess; late thirties or early forties.

"Can you talk about it now?" she asked.

He lay down beside her, threw a leg over her warm thighs. "Not here."

"Okay, let's have something to eat." She sat up.

"Now? I'm not hungry."

But the irresistible mass had been set in motion. She let his limbs drop off her and strode to the door. "We must talk," she said, walking away. "It's important."

He lay scowling at the empty doorway for a while, a recalcitrant child; then he heard the clatter of pans and decided to

197

join her. There was an odd gratification in letting her boss him around; maybe he was destined to turn into one of those men who want women to put little harnesses on them and ride them through back gardens stark naked.

She was standing behind the counter in the musical-comedy apron which seemed to serve no other purpose than to arouse him. "Why do you wear that thing?" he asked.

"I don't want my stomach splattered with boiling fat. Get me the cheese from the icebox, will you?"

He opened the door of the refrigerator. "Which one? There are four different kinds here."

"Any one. It's for with our cocktails."

"Isn't it early for cocktails?"

"Not once we start talking," she said, breaking open a box of crackers.

"I don't want to talk." He took out the Gorgonzola. "Let's let the whole thing settle before pushing it around." He closed the icebox and turned to hand her the cheese. She was staring at him; the look in her eyes was so harrowed that he asked, "What's the matter?"

She took the cheese and started to unwrap it. "I don't know what it is with you men." To his surprise, her voice was thick with tears. "What *is* it that makes you do this?"

"Do what?"

"What makes you look on death as if it were your goddam mistress?"

It threw him for a moment. Then he said, "I see your friend gave you a full report on our meeting. Charming."

"He did nothing of the sort! He just told me what you had asked him, and said you needed—"

"A naked shrink in a *Fledermaus* apron?"

"Time to recover."

"From what, for God's sake?"

"The bombing of Rauwatta! That massacre in the mountains! The fall of the Dutch East Indies! The whole mess!"

"Oh, my God!" He retreated to the dining nook.

"Haversma is a decent man, concerned about people, concerned about *you,* you ass! You're all the same! Screw you, the lot of you!"

"Well, you're off to a good start," he said pleasantly.

She threw down the box of crackers, scattering them on the counter, and stooped to get something from a drawer.

He sat down on one of the wrought-iron chairs at the glass dining table; the seat was ice cold, so he tried the banquette: better, but still chilly.

She reappeared behind the counter, put the Gorgonzola on a plate and took it together with an untidy basket of crackers to the table.

"I suggest we go back to bed," he said. "I'm getting cold."

She turned on him and shouted, "I'm trying to save your life! I'm trying to keep you from committing suicide! Don't you understand?"

"Josie," he said, after a moment, "you and Haversma are laboring under a misconception. I did not volunteer to be dropped with the paras because of a death wish, as he seems to think. I'm a journalist, it's my mission to be where the human interest is and report on it."

"Look," she said, taking off her apron, "let me try to get this through to you." She sat down on the edge of the banquette.

"Careful!" he warned. "We don't want to leave your Hungarian friend with a set of booby-traps."

She put her hands on his shoulders, pressed him down into the cushions and looked into his eyes. With those breasts dangling over him, her cause was lost before she opened her mouth.

"Let's accept the therapy," he said, "and stop quarreling over the diagnosis."

She ignored it. "What you don't know is that you aren't the only one. All volunteers in that secret training camp for para-troopers say they're motivated by patriotism, love of the Dutch East Indies, hatred of the Japs . . . "

"Well, what's wrong with that?"

"Then why enroll for commando raids that are pointless sui-cide? Why volunteer to have yourselves slaughtered for nothing, nothing at all? No one in his senses believes those raids serve any practical purpose, least of all the general who dreamed them up. He needs—"

"All right! So they don't serve any practical purpose! Men are going to be dropped, knowing they'll die: and they *volun-teered* to die! Why? It's my job to find out. What motivates them? What drove them? What are they pursuing? A dream? A vision? I think the answer is important for the future; more im-portant than any military gain that might be made."

He thought he put that rather well; the way she reacted sur-prised him. There was an incongruous tenderness in her eyes, the last thing he would have associated with Josie the single-minded hedonist. "That's a load of crap, Manny-boy," she said calmly. "The least you can do is level with yourself."

"What are you talking about? What's the matter with people here? Isn't this why every war correspondent worth his salt goes where the action is? To ferret out the human element, interpret it?"

"Manny," she said, her eyes full of that tenderness, "let me tell you something. All those guys who volunteered, and I mean *all,* are survivors, like yourself. Not one of them was evacuated in an orderly manner like the rest of us. Every one is a loner who managed to reach Australia by the skin of his teeth. You should hear their stories—one more hair-raising than the other. But all their stories have one thing in common: the one who tells it is the last to tell the tale. Every one of them is the sole survivor of a group of men who set out to try and reach Australia. There you have it."

"Have what?"

"Your motivation to volunteer is the same as theirs: not patriotism, not love of the Dutch East Indies, not hatred of the Japs, but guilt."

His heart skipped a beat. Had he mentioned it to her? He was sure he hadn't. All he had told her was the bare facts. He had not mentioned the column breaking behind his back and his failure to make the others stop. "I don't know what the hell you mean," he said. "What guilt?"

"The guilt of being alive, Manny. You carry it like a sandwich board: the anguish of a man who was saved by a miracle, or chance, while the others were killed or captured or just died by the wayside of exhaustion."

He could not hide his relief: she did not know, he had not confided in her in an unguarded moment. "Who sold you that lovely theory?" he asked. "Which chairborne jackass thought *that* up to justify his doing nothing?"

But she could not be shaken. "The only difference is in your rationalization," she continued. "You all feel responsible for what happened to the others; one says he should have stayed around instead of striking out on his own to scout the scene, another that he fell asleep while on watch, a third—well, what's yours?"

He had had time to recover. "Josie," he said, "odd as it may seem to you and your psychiatrist friend: when it comes to the nitty-gritty, I do indeed want to help recapture the Dutch East Indies. We were good to them, they were good to us; I cannot see myself dream up a fancy reason for letting others take the brunt while I sit on my ass in an office in Australia. I want to take those islands back from those murderers, those sadists with their killer dogs and their parrot voices. Not just for myself, for the natives as well."

"Don't kid yourself, Manny," she said calmly. "What we call the Dutch East Indies has always belonged to the natives. We were alien conquerors to them, now we ourselves have been conquered. We had a good run for our money; now we've been booted out, we should stay out. Certainly not pretend we want to go back for the sake of the natives." She took his hand and kissed it and held it as she said, "The natives, Manny, are going to cut your balls off and stuff 'em in your mouth after you drop out of the sky. They'll bury you alive, with only your head showing, and leave you to the ants. If you volunteer to be dropped, it means you *want* to be dead, like the rest of them. Why, Manny? Ask yourself that question. Why?"

He had to escape for a moment. He rose and made for the john.

"Where are you going?"

"Back in a minute."

Behind the closed door he sat down on the chilly seat, feeling lost and forlorn. Maybe she had made him face the truth, but it had not made him free. He experienced the waning of his inner certainty as a terrible loss. It was as if he had been allowed a glimpse of an ecstatic vision in which his whole life suddenly made sense, only to see it cloud over. Frightening how quickly the vision lost substance.

He gazed at the sampler on the opposite wall.

Some flow'rets of Eden ye still inherit, but the trail of the Serpent is over them all.

Suddenly, he was overcome by a sense of a world gone forever, of a barren emptiness ahead.

The trail of the Serpent, he reflected, was not cowardice, or stupidity, or guilt. It was war.

9

Baradja had it all worked out: she would trace the nun's lost children in the jungle around the Mission—they couldn't be far—and take them on board. Once the *Henny* was holed up in the Pond of the Dead, she and Amu would look after them until the war was over. Then the Mission would be staffed with nuns again and the children would go back there; if not, Amu and she would just keep them. Lovely for retarded children to live on a ship. Lots of things to see, lots of things to play with, always somebody around to keep an eye on them so they wouldn't run into trouble. She and Amu . . .

She went on and on, during the flight to Canberra, in the hotel room, in the limousine that took them to the Governor General's palace. Krasser listened in silence; Amu glumly nursed a cold. The fat woman, dressed up like the madame of an expensive brothel, traveled with them, rustling papers. It was a long trip.

The gala dinner at the palace was formal. The genteel contempt of the white ladies, glittering with necklaces and tiaras, for the two Dyak women was obvious. Each time she felt a sneeze coming on, Amu opened her purse, sneezed into it and closed it again.

The Governor General and some other diplomats gave flowery speeches; they made Krasser feel like an impostor again by calling him "Hero" and "Savior of the Honor of the Free World." He sat through the meal on his three cushions in silence.

When finally he and Baradja were lying in bed in the hotel and Amu emerged from the adjoining maid's room to crawl in with them, Baradja asked, "When do you think we'll sail, Benji?"

"What's the hurry?" he asked. "I thought the two of you wanted to be nurses."

"Pooh," said Amu, a small warmth in his neck.

Baradja snuggled up to him. "We didn't mean that, Benji. We want to come with you to look after those children. And you! H'm-h'm. And *him*."

This was as good a time to have it out as any other. "Listen," he said. "You've got to realize: there's almost no chance that we'll make it. Staying with me will mean the end of the line for you. I'd like you to come, but you have to know the score. So—think it over, and let me know when you've made up your minds."

They did at once. Baradja did; Amu could never stay awake more than a few minutes if he didn't want her. Her breath came in small warmths in his neck at the slow pace of sleep.

"Why are you so sure we won't make it?" Baradja asked. "We made it before."

"Look, that was a miracle. Don't you realize that? Sometime, somewhere on this trip, our luck's going to run out. I'll risk it, because I can't live in this place. You two can make a life here." That was questionable, after the way the ladies had looked at

204

them during dinner tonight; but a live *Abo* was better than a dead Dyak.

Baradja waited so long before she spoke that he thought she had fallen asleep too. Then she asked, "How much of a chance do we have, Benji?"

"One in a million," he answered. Then he remembered the nun asking him the same question; he had given her the same answer. The memory of her threatened his contentment; he put his hand on Baradja's naked buttock and it felt good. Both girls felt good, with their supple warmth snuggled up to his old body. They stood for life, for timeless rompings on the ocean sea. So he only half meant it when he said, "Baradja, that nun is like St. Elmo's Fire. What draws us is not her, but something else."

"What, Benji?"

"I don't know. But it was not white magic: the dog growling, the bird whistling at the engine, you hearing my voice calling for drinks. It was black magic, *guna-guna*. The lure of the nun, Badja, is the lure of death."

Said aloud, it sounded unconvincing. For there was his hand on her silky buttock, there were their legs thrown over his, there was Amu's breath in the nape of his neck and Baradja on his arm, full of knowledgeable lust and unsoiled righteousness. But life was life, and death was death, and somewhere the two must meet. Who was to know where or when the parallel lines would converge? Maybe they'd make it; but there was the odd feeling that had overtaken him in the limousine and during the Governor General's dinner that the lines were about to converge somewhere, soon.

Amu lay in deep sleep now, her head on his shoulder. Baradja on the other side was still awake; her eyelashes tickled his skin each time she blinked. Finally she murmured, "Benji?"

"H'm?"

"I'm sure we'll get there."

He wanted to ask her what made her so sure, but he let it

ride. She knew as much as he did about the converging lines; as a woman, she might know more. He hugged her briefly; it woke up Amu enough to kiss his shoulder, then she sank back into sleep.

Baradja started, "I think—"

"Don't think," he said. "Do what makes you feel good, don't try to work out why."

"Why not?"

"That's how you get lost. Follow your feelings, not your mind. Now sleep."

He thought she had dropped off when she mumbled, "You'll have to ask the crew—"

"I'm not going to ask the crew," he said. "I'm not about to have my life decided by a bunch of Chinese."

This time she fell asleep. As he lay there, he felt rich. Pity this newfound fullness of life would not last. But, all things considered, the thing for a man to do was to stay true to himself and to take home, to wherever he came from in the first place, the true gifts bestowed on him during his brief, turbulent life.

10

The sky was copper with the sunset and the darkening outback as vast as the ocean when Herman Winsum came riding back to his bungalow on the Harley-Davidson that went with the job. The funeral of farmer Jansen, which had taken place on the old man's own ranch, had been followed by a banquet prepared by the wives of his sons and demolished by assorted offspring, neighbors and compatriots; the editor of the *Clarion* had, of course, shared in the feast. Large amounts of whiskey and warm beer had been consumed in honor of the deceased, and now Herman was definitely sozzled. But out here, where the only danger lurking on the empty cart track might be a tardy wallaby, a drunk on a motorbike could make it home safely on condition he didn't go too fast.

It had become clear the very first day that an editor who didn't drink was considered an impostor, that only a man who could hold his liquor could be a reliable and worthy chronicler of life in Hopalong. Well, given time, he might become able to hold his own with the best. All in all, considered with a sense of humor—which was in essence a sense of proportion—he felt as happy in his new job as a snob with *Weltschmerz* could hope to be.

It was a pity, he reflected as he pushed the motorbike under the lean-to, that the plan to have himself dropped into the jungle with the paras had been crushed under the combined onslaught of Albert Haversma and Josie Bohm. It had been an idealized vision of himself which, when tested in the fires of reality, had gone up in smoke. At odd moments, especially after nightfall, alone in his corrugated-iron bungalow, with his housekeeper asleep behind the partition, banging her knee against it as she turned over, he still needed thoughts of Josie to keep him going. She had not turned up as yet; but then, she led a busy life. She wrote jolly letters with flashes of staggering frankness that made him laugh aloud in his solitude, causing his housekeeper to toss and bang her knee.

It was a healthy, virile life, with only at rare moments sudden pits of sick-making emptiness into which he seemed to fall, a damned soul, until some manifestation of reality pulled him back: the bark of a dingo outside, the distant squeal of a doomed rabbit, or the sound of his own voice: "Chin up, old boy! No glooms!"

As he came into the living room that night he found two letters propped up against the kerosene lamp.

One was from the Ministry of Agriculture, addressed to Rural Boxholder, starting: *Now the shearing season is about to commence, the following wartime restrictions have regretfully been imposed by your Government. . . .* The other was from Mrs. Josephine Bohm, Government Information Service, Consulate General of the Netherlands, Melbourne; two pages, so closely scribbled that he was forced to turn the lamp higher at the risk of setting it smoking.

Manny-boy, you really are a dingbat, sending your "Baking instructions for rolls" to the office! Don't you know that every-

body here reads everybody else's mail? Luckily, I managed to put my hands on it the moment it arrived, or Amanda Hartsuiker would have slit it open, taped it shut after reading and written on the envelope "Opened by Censor." Of course, I too am longing to have a good "roll" with you and I certainly shall, the moment I can break away. But, Snoepje, next time be more discreet in your play-by-play descriptions. Baking instructions indeed! But okay, I'll come as soon as I can. I think of you often, especially tonight, as I've just heard the news that Captain Krasser and his "Henny" have vanished from Fremantle Harbor without permission. He and his ship just evaporated into thin air. As this concerns ship movements, nobody, of course, breathes a word about it; secrecy is more than a fetish to the Dutch, it is a religion. Anyhow, good luck to him. His tarts, by the way, vanished with him; the only one he left behind is a Chinese mate, who has applied for naturalization.

As to social life here . . .

He lowered the paper.

Krasser gone! The first emotion he felt was a sense of bereavement. Not because of what might happen to Krasser, but because it felt as if part of himself, his past, had detached itself and vanished beyond the horizon. The next emotion was envy: there he went, crafty old Krasser, back to Borneo, elevating himself by that very deed to a man who could look at himself with respect. And here he sat: sodden with booze, lonely as hell, deserter from the battlefield, man without a soul.

Nonsense. No glooms! What would have been the point of having himself dropped for the Papuans to mutilate or the Japanese to slaughter? Only the harebrained notion that his presence would make a difference, however briefly, to the other white bodies about to be strewn among the rocks. Well, here at least he could do some real good: chronicle the life of a burgeoning town in the Australian outback—the weddings, the baptisms of the newborn, the progress of the sick, the eulogies for

209

the dead. He should stop fretting about his soul and mourning the waste of his wit and intellect among these empire builders as unsophisticated as their sheep. If only he could settle out here with old Bohmikins! If only she would join him in this wilderness and take him in hand!

As to social life here: Amanda Hartsuiker and Guess Who vanished together for one whole weekend and were spotted by His Excellency . . .

He read the letter to the end and concluded that the thing most precious to a man who had lost all because he had been unable to give all was hope. Who could say? She might join him after all.

He went to bed and soon fell asleep. Outside, bats gamboled among the stars. Under the lean-to, in the warm darkness, the motorbike cooled slowly with a crackling sound, like a predator of the night cracking small bones.

He dreamed vaguely of small flowers under alien stars, filled with a vague hope.

EPILOGUE

As far as the authorities could ascertain, the coaster Henny had slipped out of Fremantle Harbor under cover of darkness. Her absence was first noticed by an observant policeman late the next morning.

At first there was talk in official circles of tracking down the vessel; when none of the patrolling warships reported sighting her she was listed as "Disappeared Presumed Lost" by the minions of bureaucracy who needed an accredited formula to close their records. A ship had come, a ship had gone, that's how it went in wartime.

The reason why the search for the Henny was not pressed by the Australian Navy was that they tacitly assumed Dutch Intelligence was up to its usual tricks again. Those Hollanders played their cards close to their chests and refused to inform anyone of their covert operations in Japanese-occupied territory; they became very huffy when pressed. So, no one other than the Dutch themselves knew whether the hero of Borneo and his vessel were out on an undercover military operation or carrying bullion to Macao.

The Dutch did not contradict or confirm either supposition, and this was the beginning of the myth. When no hint was given as to the activities of the midget who had done so much to raise the Dutch flag from the mud in which it had lain trampled, people's imagination was given a free rein and rumors began to fly. By the time the war ended and the Dutch colonial empire vanished from the earth, the flight of the Henny had become a legend. Had the Indonesians been as eager to welcome back the Dutch as the Dutch had assumed, Captain Benjamin Krasser would have been given a monument, streets would have been named after him and he would have become part of the national folklore. As it happened, his story lived on only among the diminishing numbers of ex-colonials who survived the collapse of the empire.

The speed and the thoroughness with which all traces of the three centuries of Dutch rule were erased in Indonesia were as chilling to those survivors as they must have been to the citizens of Rome after the vandals sacked it and turned its glory into ashes. Because to all survivors the loss of a legend of glory diminishes their own lives, the fact that nothing was heard of the Henny after she vanished from Fremantle Harbor didn't mean, to them, that she was lost. She was never seen again and no trace of her was ever found; still, decades later, any ex-"Indischman" in his club in The Hague or Amsterdam would, after three ice-cold gins, whisper with a wink that old Krasser, the crafty rogue, had been sighted recently by a ship that lost its way in the maze of reefs off the coast of Borneo. It was said that in the swamps and the stagnant ponds of the tidal forest there could still be heard on occasion a raucous laugh, a high-pitched bark, a wolf whistle followed by the cretinous cry "I love yew!"

If so, it was the last Dutch presence in Indonesia.

About the Author

Jan de Hartog, born in Haarlem, Holland, the second son of a Calvinist minister and a Quaker mother, ran off to sea at the age of ten. At sixteen he entered Amsterdam Naval College, ending up as a junior mate in the Dutch ocean-going tugboat service. When war broke out, in 1940, and Holland was occupied by the Nazis, de Hartog was trapped in his native country. During this time he wrote and published his first major novel, *Holland's Glory,* which became an instant and historic bestseller and a symbol of the Dutch Resistance. (The German occupying forces banned the book in 1942, but it went on selling in large quantities in the underground market.) When he escaped to London in 1945, he was appointed war correspondent for the Dutch merchant marine. There he gathered the material for his postwar novels *The Distant Shore* and *The Captain,* of which over a million copies were sold in the United States alone.

In 1956 he and his wife, Marjorie, crossed the Atlantic on assignment for a number of European magazines, and after a year decided to become permanent residents of the United States. In 1962 de Hartog accepted a post as professor of English at the University of Houston, teaching creative playwriting there and at all-black Texas Southern University. His wife became a volunteer nurses' aide in the local charity hospital; de Hartog followed her and served three years as an orderly in the emergency room. Later, after publication of his book *The Hospital,* conditions in the charity hospital vastly improved and, for the first time, blacks were admitted as members to the board.

In the late sixties de Hartog, himself a Quaker, undertook the ambitious project of a multivolume novel on the history of the Religious Society of Friends. *The Peaceable Kingdom* was the first book, followed by *The Lamb's War.*

De Hartog has written many plays, among which the most famous is *The Fourposter* (later turned into the musical *I Do! I Do!*), and several volumes of essays, the best known being *A Sailor's Life* (memories of life at sea before World War II) and *The Children* (a personal record for the benefit of the adoptive parents of Asian children).

Mr. and Mrs. de Hartog live in New Jersey.